MEET THE GIRL TALK CHARACTERS

Sabrina Wells is petite, with curly auburn hair, sparkling hazel eyes, and a bubbly personality. Sabrina loves magazines, shopping, sleepovers, and most of all, she loves talking to her best friends.

Katie Campbell is a straight-A student and super athlete. With her blond hair, blue eyes, and matching clothes, she's everyone's idea of Little Miss Perfect. But Katie has a few surprises for everyone, including herself!

Randy Zak has just moved to Acorn Falls from New York City, and is she ever cool! With her radical spiked haircut and her hip New York clothes, Randy teaches everyone just how much fun it is to be different.

Allison Cloud is a Native American Indian. Allison's supersmart and really beautiful. But she has one major problem: She's thirteen years old, five foot seven, and still growing!

REBEL, REBEL

By L.E. Blair

GIRL TALK® series created by Western Publishing Company, Inc.

Western Publishing Company, Inc., Racine, Wisconsin 53404

R MCMXCIII

Text by Leah Jerome

Chapter One

"Do you believe it?" Sabrina asked us incredulously. "Sam got invited to Stacy's party!" She pushed a strand of curly red hair behind her ear. Sabs hates her hair, but I don't understand why. It's red, long, and very curly. I think it's beautiful.

We were all eating lunch in the cafeteria at Bradley Junior High School. By all, I mean Sabrina, who we usually call Sabs, Katie, Allison, who's my best friend, and me, Randy.

"Of course I don't believe it," Katie answered sympathetically. Sabs, of course, wants hair like Katie's. It's straight, light blond, and always neat. Today Katie had tied it back with a big green bow that matched her sweater. Katie is really preppie. It amazes me sometimes to think that I'm actually good friends with a preppie. Back in New York City, where I'm from, I never hung out with preps.

1

Probably because there weren't any at the small private school I went to. All the kids there were more. . .more artsy. . .or something. They're sure different from the kids here in Acorn Falls, Minnesota, where I now live with my mom.

"He *is* one of Nick's best friends," Katie continued, "and we all know that Stacy likes to think that Nick is still her boyfriend."

"I know, I know," Sabs agreed. "But, still, Sam's been totally obnoxious about it since he found out we weren't invited."

"Well, what do you expect?" I asked her. "He's just showing off." Sam is Sabrina's twin brother. They're always bickering and picking on each other, but I know they're really close. I guess it's because they're twins. Personally, I can't imagine having a sister or a brother, but having a twin might be cool. It's pretty unique and everything.

"So you can only imagine what it's like *living* with him," she sighed. "You have it made — you're an only child."

Sabs turned back to her lunch. She is always on some sort of diet or other. Not that she needs to be on a diet at all. But she thinks she could lose a few pounds. I think she reads too many of those teen magazines that always show super-thin models. I tried to tell her that top models aren't like that anymore and that they do have some meat on their bones. I mean, I should know. One of my closest friends in New York, Samantha, has been a model for five years. Sometimes, I used to go on shoots with her.

"Who wants to go to Stacy's party anyway?" asked Katie calmly. Leave it to Katie to be so logical. When I first met her at the beginning of the school year, I thought she was an ice princess. She was always so calm and so together, never showing any feelings, but that was before I got to know her. Then she really surprised me, especially when she made the boys' ice hockey team a few weeks ago. Underneath all of her polo shirts and turtlenecks, she's almost as cool as my friends back home in New York.

Anyway, Sabs, Katie, and especially Al are the nicest part about Acorn Falls. We are definitely a strange group, for Bradley Junior High anyway. Al is a Native American, a real Chippewa Indian. I think that's kind of cool. I thought that, living in New York City, you could meet anybody, but I had never met a real Native American before.

My mom and I moved out here in June after my parents got divorced. My mom grew up here and said she wanted to "get back to her roots" for a year. I could have handled it if her roots were in Long Island or somewhere a little closer to home. But Acorn Falls is so far away.

I have to admit that I didn't like it when we first got here. I was used to all the action in New York, and everything seemed so quiet in Acorn Falls. I mean, if you want to buy a magazine or a pack of gum on Sunday, when all the stores on Main Street are closed, you have to get in your car and drive somewhere. That's really weird. And I still can't believe that Acorn Falls actually has a street called Main Street. It's like out of *Tom Sawyer*, or something.

Things got better when I met Sabrina, Katie, and Allison, although I still want to go back to New York in June. I miss my friends back there, especially Sheck. But Sheck is coming to Acorn Falls to visit me for Thanksgiving.

I can't wait.

Just then Allison broke into my thoughts.

"I can't wait to get started on my English paper," she said as she opened her brown lunch bag. She always brings lunch from home. One thing about Allison that I can't get used to, though, is that she's always doing her homework or thinking about doing her homework. "What are you guys doing yours on?" she asked.

"I'm going to do *Tom Sawyer*," Katie said.

Sabs groaned. I almost joined her. I couldn't believe the two of them were talking about homework during lunch. It almost seemed unnatural.

"What do you think about Stacy's party, Al?" Sabs asked, changing the subject.

"You mean *the* party of the year?" Allison responded, smiling. I think she likes to tease Sabs once in a while. I do, too. But Sabs takes social things so seriously. Sometimes you just have to laugh. But she knows we're only kidding.

"Well, I wasn't invited," Allison admitted. "Were any of you invited?" she asked, as if a sudden thought had struck her.

Katie giggled. "Well, Al, I was invited but I didn't want to tell anyone."

Sabrina started laughing, and I joined in. I mean, the thought of Stacy "the Great" Hansen inviting any of us to her boy-girl party was just too funny.

Stacy's one of those people who truly believes she is a princess or something. Just because her father is the principal, she walks around as if she owns the school. I guess some people think she's pretty. But I think she's kind of run-of-the-mill. I mean, there's nothing unusual about her. She has long blond hair, and big brown eyes, and she was the first girl in the seventh grade to wear a bra — believe me, she let everyone know about that. But she looks like she belongs on car commercials to me.

Anyway, Stacy definitely has something against all of us. I also think she's totally jealous of Sabs. Everybody loves Sabs, and she has a ton of friends. I really don't know how she does it. I guess it's because she's so nice to everyone and they always want to talk to her. It takes me a while to warm up to people most of the time. And forget it if I'm in a bad mood.

I don't think Sabs has bad moods. I mean, she gets depressed once in a while, but it passes quickly.

"She has the grossest clothes," Eva Malone announced loudly from a few tables away. I didn't have to look around to see who she was talking about — it was obviously me.

Eva is one of Stacy the Great's friends. Stacy has three of them, and we call them her clones. Eva is Stacy's best friend, and by far the most obnoxious. Everybody calls her "Jaws" because her mouth's full of braces.

Anyway, I saw Allison begin to tense up. She hates confrontations. Sabs and Katie just looked at me. Then Sabs started to stand up. She always has to be first to stick up for anyone, even if she can't think of a good comeback line. But I didn't need anyone to fight my battles.

"It's okay, Sabs," I said, getting her to sit down.

"What's with the color black?" Laurel Spencer asked loudly. "Does she think she's at a funeral or something?" I was surprised at that one. Laurel is the true ice queen. She never says anything at all — just freezes you out. So this was definitely an occasion.

I looked down at my outfit. I couldn't understand why they were making any kind of commotion about it at all. It wasn't my most bizarre, that's for sure. I had on a black turtleneck and an old black vest of my father's. For a skirt, I had on a black knit tube — the kind that can be pulled up to make a dress or worn short for a skirt. I also wore black granny boots that laced up my calf, and black tights. I thought I looked cool. I really couldn't understand why Stacy the Great and her clones were making such a fuss about the whole thing today.

Meanwhile, the four of them were wearing a startling array of pastels. Stacy, of course, was wearing pink and green. I hate pink. She had on a mint-green sweater with these things that looked like pale pink cotton balls stuck all over the yoke, mint-green socks, and a pink skirt. Laurel was wearing light blue. It suited an ice queen like her. Eva was wearing a pale yellow sweater dress that made her look kind of like an underripe banana. And B.Z. Latimer was wearing a peach jump suit.

Sabrina says that B.Z.'s not so bad when she's not around Stacy, but Sabs always looks for the best in everyone. She says that I always see the worst. I suppose she's right in a way.

"And that hat is really gauche," I heard Stacy say. Stacy must have just learned that word, because she pronounced it wrong. It should be "goh-shh" not "gaw-shay." I guess I forgot to mention my hat. It's black, of course, with a wide brim, and falls down over my eyes. I think it's kind of hip.

"It's better than looking like a box of tissues, hmm?" I said loudly to no one in particular. "Or maybe pastel-colored cotton balls," I added.

Stacy spluttered a little, and a few people near us laughed at my remark. Stacy hates to be laughed at. I didn't hear anything else out of her or her clones after my brilliant comeback. I love driving them all crazy.

"Well, now look at what you've done, Randy," Sabs said, trying to keep from smiling. That's another thing I like about Sabs — she's got a sense of humor about everything. I don't understand how she can find something to laugh about all the time. "You've really blown our chances," she continued. "We'll never be invited to Stacy's party now."

I laughed, since we all knew it wasn't very likely that Stacy would invite any of us to her party in the first place.

Just then the bell rang, and the four of us jumped up to clear our trays and get to our next classes in time. I'm just not used to all these bells, and rules, and stuff. My school in New York was very unstructured compared to here. In a lot of ways I really miss New York City.

Chapter Two

After school, Katie, Sabs, Allison, and I stopped off at Fitzie's, the hangout for junior high kids. Fitzie's is great. It's always packed, and it's a real neighborhood kind of place. There's nothing like it back in New York as far as I know.

It had begun to get dark when I started skateboarding home. I still can't get used to how early it gets dark in Acorn Falls. It seems darker here than it ever did in New York. But maybe that's because there aren't exactly a ton of streetlights in Acorn Falls. Not like on Fifth Avenue, where it looks like noon at midnight.

Anyway, I was glad it was Friday. Every Friday my mother and I rent a good "chop-'em-up" horror movie and eat takeout Chinese food. I love Chinese food. Ho Lin's in Acorn Falls is pretty good, even if it doesn't compare to Chinatown in New York. Anyway, there is no better way to start a weekend than by watching horror movies and eating Chinese food. At least that tradition hasn't changed since we moved out here.

I crouched lower on my skateboard to gain more speed. I remembered how strange my skateboarding seemed to everyone here in the beginning. I guess most girls in Acorn Falls don't do this sort of thing. But Sheck, who's my best friend in New York, and I used to skateboard everywhere. We were definitely sidewalk terrors. With such wide open spaces out here, I think it's funny that more kids don't use skateboards.

I don't know what I'm going to do about my skateboard when it snows. It snowed a little earlier this month, and it was murder having to take the bus. Everyone keeps telling me it was nothing compared to the typical snowfall in Minnesota. It's going to be a long winter without my skateboard.

I rounded the corner onto my street, Maple Street, and pulled into my driveway. Our house is not really a house. It's a big, old converted barn. In New York I lived in a huge apartment called a loft. I guess I can still say

I've never lived in a house. Anyway, it's a great barn. Practically the whole ceiling is a skylight. My mom is an artist and needs the light for her work.

I popped my skateboard into the air, caught it on its way down, and ran up the steps to the front door.

"M!" I called as I slammed the door shut. Sabs, Katie, and Allison think it's strange that I call my mother M, but I've called Mom that for as long as I remember. "M" is a nickname for "Mom." I call my father "D" for "Dad." Everyone was really surprised when M said they should call her by her first name, which is Olivia. She's always hated being called Mrs. Zak, and my friends in New York call her Olivia, too. I try not to laugh, though, when my friends make a point of not calling her anything at all. Except for Sabs. Sabs loves calling her Olivia. I think it makes her feel grown-up.

"In here, Ran!" my mother called from the right side of the barn, where she has her studio. I dropped my bag, jacket, and skateboard at the door and headed back there.

"Hey, this is really good!" I exclaimed, looking at her latest painting. She is really good. I still can't get over it. M didn't paint much when we lived in New York. My father is a video and television producer, and I guess he has to socialize a lot. They went out all the time and till all hours. M calls it "schmoozing." Now that she's away from New York and here in Acorn Falls, she's been painting up a storm. She told me that she was an art student in New York when she first met my father, and she dropped out to marry him. She's finally picked up where she left off, and her career has zoomed.

"Thanks, Ran," my mother said, brushing back a lock of her hair, which is the same jet black as mine and just as wild. I noticed that she had splotches of blue paint all over her face. "Hey, listen," she said. "I'm going to do a few more minutes here and then I'll clean up. Why don't you order something from Ho Lin's, and I'll go pick it up when it's ready."

"Sounds good," I called over my shoulder, and I headed to the other side of the barn where the kitchen is. My mother's bedroom is an area next to the kitchen. She put up huge Chinese screens around the space to separate it from the kitchen and the living room. My room is in a loft above the kitchen. It's kind of small, but I love it. It's funny how my mother knew that I needed more privacy than screens and gave me the loft. But my mother is always surprising me.

I felt like having something new and different so I ordered shrimp and snow peas, twice-cooked pork, and sesame chicken. Then I started cleaning the kitchen. When M gets into a painting, she forgets about everything else. After I washed all the dishes in the sink and cleaned off the counters, I decided to start the laundry. Like I said, my mother just forgets stuff like housework, but I don't mind. I don't know how Katie or Al put up with their mothers telling them to pick up their stuff all the time. I couldn't handle it. I like doing things when I want to do them. It's weird, though: In New York we had a cleaning lady come in every day, so I never noticed that my mother never did housework. But since the divorce I feel kind of responsible for her, so I try to keep the house from falling apart.

Forty-five minutes later, my mother and I were sitting in our living room. I sat on one antique brocade love seat and she sat on the other one. All of our furniture here is antique. M says she likes stuff with a history better than new stuff. New stuff was all we had in our apartment back in New York. Everything there was black leather and chrome. My father says the style is called Italo-modern or something like that. He thinks it's the best, but I guess my mother never did. Lucky for him that his new girlfriend, Leighton, seems to like it just fine.

We had rented two great movies — *Lunch Meat* and *Pumpkinhead*. I'm lucky my mom shares the same warped appreciation for bad horror movies that I do.

"Listen, Randy," M began excitedly, through a mouthful of fried rice. "Did I tell you that the gallery in Minneapolis wants to feature me in its show on area artists in January? I can't believe it! I am so excited."

"That's great!" I exclaimed. I was really excited for her. She'd been working so hard since we'd been here. It was wonderful to know it was finally paying off.

"And then they told me that, depending on how the show goes, they may want me to do a one-woman show next fall!" my mother went on.

Next fall! I thought to myself. "But we won't be here then," I said, confused. "Are you going to fly back here or something?"

M didn't say anything at first. She just looked down at her plate of Chinese food. "M?" I asked, getting a little worried.

"Well, Ran, I guess I was hoping that we'd still be here," she said softly.

"What?" I exclaimed. I couldn't believe this! We had to go back to New York. It was home.

"You know, Randy, you have been happy here," my mother said. "You've made a lot of new friends, and you're doing well in school. I was really worried about you when we first moved out here, but you seem to have adjusted fine. And my painting is going so well. I think if we went back to New York, I would lose all this peace and wouldn't be able to paint."

"But we don't belong here!" I cried. I knew I could never fit in here permanently. A year was one thing, but forever was something totally different.

"Come on, Randy, give it a chance," my mother urged. "I thought Sabs, Katie, and

Allison were your good friends. And, besides, a change of scenery is very healthy. Don't worry. You'll still get to see your father ... and ... Leighton."

I find it hard to believe that my father has this new girlfriend already, but my mother just said, "Whatever makes him happy." I guess that's easier for my mother to say in Minnesota, but it would be harder for her to be happy for him if she was in New York.

I met Leighton when I went to stay with my father over Labor Day weekend. She's young, blond, and pretty. My father produced her in a few commercials before they started going out. She's nothing like my mother. She also had nothing to do with their divorce. I think she's okay, not great, but okay. I just didn't like the fact that when I was with them, it seemed as if everywhere D and I went, Leighton was always with us. I didn't have my father to myself for one minute. Not that Leighton was mean to me or anything. She was just always there. I couldn't deal with it. I ended up coming back to Acorn Falls a day early. I never told my mother why.

"Randy," my mother said gently, passing

me a fortune cookie. "I'm not going to force you to stay. You know how I feel, but I would never do anything to make you miserable. So just think about it, and we'll talk about it again. It's a long time until June."

I broke open my fortune cookie and slowly pulled out the piece of paper inside.

"What does yours say?" my mother asked me.

"'Change makes the world go around,'" I replied slowly. "What a stupid fortune." The fortunes in New York were always much better.

"I don't think that's stupid, Randy," my mother said. "Here, listen to mine: 'You will soon reap the rewards of your creativity.'"

"Great," I muttered. I didn't feel like talking anymore. I didn't care if change made the world go around. I hate change.

Fortunately, the horror movies we had chosen were particularly good. I got so interested in them that I forgot all about living in Acorn Falls and never going back to New York.

Afterward I went up to my room and got ready for bed. I put on an old ripped-up white button-down shirt of my father's that is one of my favorites. Then I lay on my big old cast-iron bed that we found at an antique store, and I stared at the ceiling. What was I going to do? I really, really wanted to go back to New York. But my mother really wanted to stay in Acorn Falls.

I looked around at the mess in my room. I've never been a neat person. There was stuff lying all over the place: books, papers, shoes, jeans. I looked at the painting hanging on the wall opposite my bed. My mom painted it for me when I was little. It's a panoramic view of Central Park in the winter in the snow. Looking at it reminded me of going sledding there with my dad when I was small. It's a great painting. Maybe if I wished hard enough, I could find myself back in New York. I couldn't imagine spending my life in Acorn Falls. I am New York born and bred. I could live with my father, I guess. But then I'd have to deal with Leighton every day, and I would really miss my mom. I just didn't know what to do. I thought things were supposed to get easier as you got older — not harder.

Chapter Three

I woke up to my alarm ringing. I have one of those old-fashioned clocks, with the bells on top. I practically need a train running through my room to get me up in the morning. M was screaming at me from downstairs to turn it off. It must have woken her up, too. That happens a lot, since I am capable of sleeping through the loudest ringing for hours. I'm glad she's not a morning person either.

I rolled over slowly and flipped the lever on the top of the clock. Then I turned over onto my back and tried to focus. Looking around my little room, I saw my drum set in the corner. My dad bought me my first drum when I was six, and I've been playing ever since. I felt like playing my drums because whenever I have a problem, playing my drums always makes me feel better. And the possibility of never living in New York again was definitely a major problem. But that would drive M crazy, so I just lay there.

Suddenly, my eyes popped open. The mall! I was gong to be late. I was meeting Sabs, Katie, and Al at the mall, and we were going to see a movie. We go to the mall almost every Saturday. I didn't feel like going, but I didn't see any way to get out of it. I hate having to go out when I'm feeling confused about something. I don't want to talk to anyone. I don't want to see anyone. Most people don't understand that when you have a problem, sometimes you have to think it through before you talk to anyone. I had a feeling that Sabs and Katie and maybe even Al wouldn't understand it if I spent the afternoon not talking.

I knew they were counting on me, so I sat up and let my feet hit the floor. One of the things I really like about my room is the floor. The wood is old and dark brown, and I have this cool throw rug, with a geometric pattern, that covers just the middle part of the floor. Back in New York, my room had wall-to-wall carpeting in some designer color like seafoam green or something. It was okay, but I like wood better. It's more solid, somehow.

I shuffled over to the door and headed downstairs to the shower. I'm always a little more human after a shower. After I showered, I dressed in my favorite jeans, my granny boots, and another old white shirt of my father's that I buttoned all the way up to the neck. Then I went back downstairs to get breakfast.

"Morning, Ran," my mother greeted me as I walked into the kitchen. She was busy scrambling eggs. "How'd you sleep?"

It was obvious to me that something was bothering her, too, because she was cooking. She only cooks when something is wrong. M's always been a takeout kind of person.

"Okay," I said as I plopped down in a chair. I didn't feel like saying anything more. Why would my mother want to stay here? That wasn't part of our deal. Why did she have to make things so complicated?

We were both silent as my mother cooked, humming to the old Simon and Garfunkel album on the stereo. We always have music on in our house. M usually lets me play my music on our CD player, as long as it's at an acceptable noise level. I think parents' ears get more sensitive as they get older, though, because her acceptable level is very different from mine.

Anyway, M was definitely upset if she was playing Simon and Garfunkel. That's all she listened to over the summer right after the divorce. She said it reminded her of happier times. Personally, when I'm upset, I'd rather listen to loud music. Mellow music is just too depressing. This morning I felt like some serious head-banging tunes.

"So are you going to the mall today?" M asked me, in a fake-cheerful voice.

"Yes," I answered. I didn't feel like getting into it.

"Do you need a ride?"

"Yes, I guess so," I said, hoping she'd realize how down I felt. I couldn't help thinking how great everything would be at this moment if she would only stick to the original plan.

After a pretty silent breakfast, I grabbed my black leather bomber jacket and my skateboard and ran out to the car. My mom knows when to push the talking issue and when not to. I guess she could tell that today was not the day to continue our mother-daughter chat about our future. I know she hates to see me upset, but I didn't know what to do about it right then. I needed time to think.

When M dropped me at the mall, Allison and Katie were sitting outside of Dare, Sabs's favorite store. Of course, Sabrina wasn't there yet. That girl is always late. She even sets her watch ahead fifteen minutes so she can get to places on time, but it never works. I plopped down next to them on the bench.

"Hey, Randy," Katie greeted me.

"Hi," Allison said softly.

I just nodded. It was going to be a long day if I couldn't even exchange basic greetings.

My mother tells me I give out very strong vibes. She says she can always read my moods, so she knows when to leave me alone. I always thought she was making fun of me, but maybe she's right, because Allison and Katie sure weren't trying to chat with me today.

"Where's Sabs?" I finally grunted after about five minutes of sitting there in total silence.

"Who knows?" Katie answered, sighing. "You know how she is. She even called me this morning to tell me to try to get here earlier so she would have more time to shop before the movie. Can you believe it?"

Allison chuckled. "I believe it," she said. "But that's just the way she is. It won't do any good to get impatient, Randy."

Allison is almost as great at reading me as my mother. She must have known I was getting more and more impatient with each passing second. But that's the way I've always been. I hate waiting for anything or anyone. It drives me crazy. I couldn't understand how she could just sit there so calmly. Didn't she ever get anxious?

"So what movies did you and your mother see last night?" Katie asked me.

That was definitely the wrong question. It started me thinking about my mother and Acorn Falls and New York all over again. "I don't remember," I answered. I didn't mean to be short with her, but that whole issue was very sensitive for me.

"What do you mean, you don't remember?" Katie asked. "How can you not remember? You just saw them last night."

Leave it to Katie to be so logical. I didn't want to remember, because then I'd have to think about M wanting to stay in Acorn Falls forever.

Luckily, Allison changed the subject and got Katie talking about the English paper. I just sat there not thinking at all. I tried to make my mind blank the way you're supposed to do in certain Eastern religions when you're trying to attain inner peace. It didn't work.

Finally Sabs came running up to us. "You'll never believe it!" she exclaimed.

"What?" Katie asked, looking up at Sabs intently.

"Stacy is inviting eighth graders to her party, too," Sabrina said excitedly.

"I can't believe it," Katie said. "The biggest party of the year, and we're not even invited."

"You know," Sabs said, looking thoughtful, "I bet Stacy just wants to make me mad."

"Well, you are, aren't you?" I asked, a little impatiently.

Sabs looked startled and turned to me. "I'm not mad, Randy," she said, sounding a bit miffed. "I'm just upset that we're going to miss all the fun. Having a party to go to on the Friday after Thanksgiving would be great."

"I don't know," Katie admitted. "Maybe we

could go ice-skating or something."

Sabs grimaced. Her facial expressions crack me up. Sabs's face is definitely a reflection of her feelings. She can't hide anything.

The idea of ice-skating didn't thrill me anyway. I had just learned to ice-skate. Katie taught me. She's really great on the ice. I'm not so good yet. I have to admit that I hate doing anything I'm not good at. I like to be the best at everything.

"I have plans already," I said, suddenly remembering that my friend Sheck was going to be around then. I knew that the two of us would definitely find something different to do — even in Acorn Falls.

"Oh, that's right," Allison said. "Your friend from New York is going to be here, isn't he?"

Sabs and Katie turned toward me. "That's right," Sabs agreed. "Your friend from New York. What's his name again? It's something weird, isn't it?"

Sabs's face was showing her feelings again. She wanted to know all about this new boy.

"Sheck," I answered. "He's been my best friend forever. He lives in the apartment next door to mine — I mean, next door to my father's."

"Well, when's he coming?" asked Katie.

"My mother and I are going to get him at the airport after school on Monday. He's going to stay until Sunday night," I replied. Suddenly I didn't feel so bad. I was really excited by the thought that I'd be seeing Sheck again. I hadn't seen him in nearly six months. The last time I talked to him, he told me he had grown three and a half inches. My friend Samantha told me he's a total hunk this year in school. I can't see Sheck as a hunk. Samantha must be going nuts or something — probably because I'm not there.

"I've never had a boy for a best friend," Katie said. "What's it like?"

"I don't know," I said quickly. "It's like being friends with anyone else, I guess. Sheck and I talk about the same things we talk about."

"Really!" Sabs exclaimed. "Even other boys?"

"I don't really talk about boys, Sabs," I said. "You do."

Sabs looked hurt for a moment, but then

Allison, once again, changed the subject. I guess Allison and I are such good friends because I always seem to say the wrong thing and get people mad. Then Allison says the right thing, and everyone is happy again. It's a symbiotic relationship. I learned that word in science class. It means when two things are totally dependent on each other to survive. Sometimes I think Al and I are like that.

"Do you guys want to go into Dare before we go to the movie?" Allison asked.

Sabs jumped up. "Oh, they're having a big sale. Let's go see what they've got. We have almost half an hour before the movie starts."

So, even though I felt like just sitting there, or just getting on my skateboard and skating away from the mall at top speed, I got up and followed them into Dare. It was packed with people.

Allison and I wandered away from Sabs and Katie, who were pawing through the large, overstuffed sale rack. Neither of us were into shopping. Allison doesn't really care about clothes. And I can't get used to malls. I hate enclosed shopping areas. I like the little shops and stores of Greenwich Village, in downtown New York better.

Just then I heard a loud shriek of laughter coming from the dressing room. It sounded an awful lot like Sabs. I looked across the room to the sale rack where she and Katie had been standing. They were nowhere in sight. It could only mean trouble. Sabs is always doing this to us.

"What do you think, guys?" Sabs asked Allison and me as she stepped out into the store. "Is it me?"

I laughed. I couldn't help it. Sabs was wearing a long, strapless silver dress that was about four sizes too large for her. She had her T-shirt on underneath it.

"I know I have to fill out a little," Sabs continued, pulling at the extra foot of fabric at the top that kept falling down. "But I'm hoping to do that before Friday, so if Stacy invites us to her party, I'll have something really special to wear."

I couldn't stop laughing. Sabs looked so funny. She's so short and the dress was so long and so large. She could probably have fitted another person or two in that dress along with her.

"I'm not sure the color is right for you," Allison commented, grinning at me. "I think gold might set off the highlights in your hair better."

"Allison, the model, speaks," Katie put in, as she came up behind Sabs. "She does have a point. Maybe you should try on something else."

Sabs agreed and headed back into the dressing room. Two minutes later she was back.

"What do you think, guys?" Sabs asked, spinning in front of us. "Is this me?"

I couldn't believe what she was wearing now. She looked like one big human ruffle. I guess it was supposed to be a dress, but it was hard to tell. It was a neon Hawaiian print in green, pink, and orange with rows of ruffles on the bottom and on the top. I had never seen anything like it.

I started laughing again and so did Al and Katie. Pretty soon we were all in total hysterics. I actually started to cry. That happens to me sometimes when I laugh too much. Meanwhile Sabs kept spinning around, trying to act really serious about the whole thing. It's amazing how Sabs can make everyone laugh.

"Hey, guys," Katie said, trying to regain control. "We better get moving if we're going to make the movie."

Sabs ran off to change, and Katie bought a pair of socks. Then we all walked out into the mall.

The four of us took the escalator up to the movie theaters. Sabs bought a jumbo-sized box of popcorn for us to share, and we filed into the theater. We always have a major debate about where to sit. Sabs likes to sit in the very front. The rest of us can't stand craning our necks. I like to sit all the way in the back. That way, you can see what everyone else in the theater is doing. Allison and Katie like to sit in the middle, of course. So we always have a discussion about where to go, and we always end up sitting in the middle. Today was no exception.

I was actually looking forward to seeing the movie, but then the credits started to roll. I couldn't believe it. The movie opened in New York. It even looked as if it had been filmed just blocks away from my school. Everything seemed very familiar. Suddenly I felt incredibly homesick.

I couldn't live in this town forever! I was not an Acorn Falls type of person. I mean, I liked my friends and all, but I wasn't supposed to stay here forever. Why didn't my mother understand that? I couldn't leave her, but I couldn't stay here. What was I going to do? I knew my mother was counting on me. One thing was for sure, I couldn't sit and watch this movie anymore. I pulled my skateboard out from under my seat and stood up.

"Where are you going?" Katie whispered.

Sabs dragged her eyes away from the screen. A man was spying on a woman in a fur coat who was walking down a street that looked like it was on the Upper West Side in New York. "What are you doing?" she asked.

"I'm leaving," I announced a little too loudly. The couple four rows back shushed me.

"What's wrong?" Katie asked. "Why are you leaving?"

"I've got things to do," I answered shortly, getting another "Shush" from the back. "I'll see you guys later."

I stalked up the aisle. I could hear Sabs asking, "What's wrong with her?" And then I heard Katie ask if they should come after me. Luckily, Allison told them to sit down and let me go. Thank goodness for Allison and the way she understands me. I had to get out of there and skateboard for a while. I felt like I was suffocating.

Chapter Four

"You better hurry, Ran," my mother called up to my room. "You'll be late for school."

I didn't really care if I was late for school or not. I actually thought about pretending to be sick. I hadn't seen Allison, Sabs, or Katie since Saturday afternoon, when I ran out of the movie. I was sure that they would want to know what was wrong with me. I'd been dodging their calls all weekend — mostly because I just didn't know what to say. I know they mean well and everything, but I didn't feel like explaining the whole thing yet. None of them had a clue that I might be staying in Acorn Falls permanently.

I thought about how the day would just drag by if I stayed in bed, so I got up. Sheck's plane was coming in at eight o'clock that night, and I couldn't wait.

My mother was nowhere in sight when I

got downstairs. I hoped I could get out of the house without seeing her because I really didn't feel like talking. Yesterday I just wanted to watch football. The New York Giants were playing the Minnesota Vikings. I didn't have any loyalty problem about who to root for — I'm a Giants fan all the way. That will never change.

Anyway, during the game my mother kept bringing me popcorn and stuff. Then later she got us a pizza for dinner, with pepperoni on it, which I love, even though she thinks pepperoni is really bad for me. She was being so nice, and I was being such a grump.

When the game was over, my mother came into the living room and asked me if I wanted to pose for her. She wanted to do a portrait of me for her show in January. M used to sketch and paint me a lot when I was younger. She hadn't done anything like that in a long time.

First she had me straddle one of the kitchen stools. She likes to draw people in what she considers the poses most natural to them. She said that sitting like that was "very me," though I don't see why.

I began to feel really good sitting there,

very still, watching her stare at me and then draw. It was so peaceful and quiet. I began to feel that things weren't so bad. I know I'm lucky to have M for a mother. She really tries to understand me and what I'm going through. Sometimes I actually feel as if she's more like a friend than a mother.

It wasn't until I was lying in bed later that night that I'd started thinking about the whole New York versus Acorn Falls thing again. I had to make a decision soon. But it was really hard, since there were pros and cons on both sides. I tossed and turned all night worrying.

This morning I still felt worried as I went down to the kitchen to make breakfast. I looked through the kitchen cupboards and even under the sink, where my mother sometimes puts things by mistake. The only breakfast foods we had were oat bran or granola. Some choice. I decided on the oat bran. M showed up halfway through my bowl of cereal.

"Morning, hon," she greeted me as she headed for the refrigerator. She pulled out the lactose-free milk she likes. I don't know how she can drink that stuff. I'm glad she hadn't stopped buying me regular milk — even if it is skim. I don't think I could handle cereal without milk, especially oat bran.

"Morning," I mumbled, picking up my still half-full bowl of cereal. I didn't feel like finishing it now. I carried it over to the sink and turned to leave.

"Ran, you didn't finish your cereal," my mother said, concerned. "Are you feeling all right?"

"Yeah," I answered. "Don't worry about it. I'm just not hungry."

"Okay," she said, looking at me as if she wanted to say something more.

I ran upstairs and grabbed my books, jacket, and skateboard. I had to get out of the house, even if it meant going to school. On my way out, my mother reminded me that we had to leave by seven o'clock that night to get to the airport on time to pick up Sheck.

It was really cold outside, and I could see my breath as I skateboarded down the sidewalk toward school. It was probably going to snow soon. Al told me once that she usually knows when it's going to snow. Allison can predict the weather. It's kind of bizarre how she always knows what the next day will be like. Anyway, she said there's a kind of stillness to the air, as there was now. I just hoped it would hold off until after eight o'clock, so we could pick up Sheck without any problems.

It was early when I got to school, and the halls were still kind of empty. I saw Allison sitting at a table in the library. I didn't feel like talking, so I ran by without saying hello.

After I got my books out of my locker, I went into the stairwell and sat down on a window ledge. I put my Walkman on and stared outside at the football field. Things were so different here. In New York, when I looked out the school windows, all I could see was a concrete playground and basketball court and a lot of apartment buildings. My school didn't even have a football team. It was totally different from Bradley. I mean, Katie, Sabs, and Allison are really good friends and all, and I'll miss them a lot, but I have to go back to New York. I belong there.

I can't help it if I can't get into the cheerleading, the dances, the football games, and the parades — all the stuff that is so important here. I'd rather spend my Sundays at a new photography exhibit downtown than in the bleachers watching the Wolves score touch-downs. Suddenly I made up my mind once and for all. I had to go back to New York. I was just going to have to tell my mother tonight. And then I'd have to tell my friends. I had no idea how I would explain it to them, though, without hurting their feelings.

I decided to find Allison. I needed to talk to somebody. When I walked into the library, Allison was just where I'd seen her earlier.

"Hey, Al," I greeted her, as I sat down in a chair opposite her. "How's it going?"

Allison looked up, startled. When she gets into a book, she totally forgets about her sur-roundings. I think she could probably read through a rock concert.

"Hi, Randy," she answered. "How are you? We were all worried after what happened at the movies on Saturday." She let her voice trail off. I could tell by the concerned look in her eyes that she really just wanted to know if I was okay, but she also didn't want to pry.

"I've just got a lot on my mind, Al," I said with a sigh.

All of a sudden we heard shouts from the

hallway.

"We better get going so we're not late for first period," Allison said, as she gathered her books together. "You know, Randy," she said softly, "I'm always here if you ever need to talk."

"I know," I replied quickly. Allison really was a good friend. How could I go back to New York and leave her and Sabs and Katie behind?

The morning went by pretty quickly. I had brought my lunch with me — a vanilla yogurt and a box of raisins. I decided to eat outside by myself even though it was cold. The sun was out, though, and I just had to be alone for a few minutes to clear my head. I wasn't in the mood to chat with Katie and Sabs and Al — not yet anyway.

I didn't run into any of them until social studies, seventh period. I sit right behind Sabs in that class because of alphabetical order. She got there late, as usual. She tapped me on the shoulder as she slid into her seat, and I smiled at her, but we didn't have a chance to talk.

Our teacher, Mr. Grey, was out for the week, so we had a substitute named Mr.

Delafield. He had three double chins and wore a floppy brown toupee. Sam told us that his nickname is "the Rug." A rug is slang for a bad toupee, by the way. Anyway, the Rug was droning on and on about the battles of Lexington and Concord. Boring.

"What happened when the British marched into Concord?" Mr. Delafield asked. I stared out the window. "Rowena Zak?" he said, looking up from the seating chart on his desk.

I looked away from the window and up at him. "I don't know," I said, startled that he had called on me. I was so lost in thought that I didn't even bother to tell him that my name was Randy. I honestly didn't know the answer, and when I don't know something, I don't like to guess.

I heard somebody in the front row laugh.

"It was in the reading, Miss Zak," Mr. Delafield went on. Why wouldn't he leave me alone? I didn't know. I hadn't done the reading. I had more important things on my mind than some social studies reading. Why couldn't this place be more progressive, like my old school? The teachers there wanted to encourage creativity, so we never had to do anything we didn't want to. We spent a lot of time on independent projects.

"Didn't you do the reading, Rowena?" Mr. Delafield continued as he walked toward the back of the room to stand in front of my desk.

"No," I replied. "I'm sorry. I forgot." Why did he have to stand right in front of my desk? His toupee looked really bad up close. It kind of tilted to one side.

"And why not?" he asked. "I'm sure the class would be very interested in what was so much more important than your homework."

Who did this man think he was? Just because he was a teacher, I had to tell him, and the class, all my problems? Give me a break. There was no chance of that. I didn't say anything. Besides, I had forgotten all about the reading because of all the other things running through my mind. Mr. Grey would have understood. He was really cool about stuff like missed readings.

"I'm sure nobody in this class would care," I mumbled.

"Pardon me," the Rug said obnoxiously. "I didn't hear your answer. Maybe you didn't understand my question."

I just stared at him without saying a word. I had already told him I didn't know. His standing over me was not going to make me think of the answer. Anyway, why couldn't he just call on someone else? I knew I should have done the homework, but I hadn't.

"Well?" Mr. Delafield said.

"I don't know," I repeated.

I heard someone else laugh.

"Go to the principal's office this instant!" the Rug suddenly barked at me.

I could see Sabs flinching in front of me, but I didn't move.

"Did you hear me, young lady?" Mr. Delafield practically yelled.

I carefully gathered up my books and closed my notebook. I stood up and walked slowly out of the room. Bradley Junior High was the most ridiculous school I'd ever been in. I really couldn't wait to get back to New York. I mean, what did he want from me? I wasn't trying to cause any trouble.

Three other kids were outside Mr. Hansen's office when I got there. I sat down at the end of the line. I hunched down in my seat, pulled out my Walkman, and turned the volume practically all the way up.

Fifteen minutes later I walked into Mr. Hansen's office. He gave me detention for that afternoon. I couldn't believe it — detention! And I had to get ready to pick up Sheck. Forget Acorn Falls and forget all these silly people. I was going back to New York.

My last-period class, math, passed in a blur. I had no idea what anyone was talking about. Luckily, the teacher didn't call on me. If they had, I probably would have gotten double detention or something like that. We didn't even have detention in my old school. They thought the concept was too negative and old-fashioned.

I was a minute late for detention. And the proctor was Mr. Delafield. Just my luck. He raised his eyebrow at me when I walked in, and pulled out the detention slips.

"Looking for another afternoon here, Miss Zak?" he asked, as I sat down. The room was pretty deserted. There were only five other people in the classroom. I remembered seeing three of them at the office when I was there.

"No," I said, shortly, and opened my notebook. I had to write "I will not disrupt the class and prevent the other students from learning" five hundred times. What a weird punishment. What does writing a sentence five hundred times teach anyone?

Finally, I finished and handed the paper in to Mr. Delafield. I ran out of school and hopped on my skateboard and headed home. I couldn't wait until we went to the airport to pick up Sheck. Suddenly I remembered I was going to have to tell my mother that I wanted to move back to New York. That thought slowed me down because I had a definite feeling that it wasn't exactly going to go over big.

Chapter Five

The phone rings just before Randy and her mother are supposed to leave for the airport.

MRS. ZAK: Randy! It's Allison.

ALLISON: Hi, Randy?

RANDY: Yup.

ALLISON: Listen, I know you want us to leave you alone, but I just wanted to tell you that Sabs, Katie, and I are really worried about you.

RANDY: Well, you don't have to be. Everything's fine.

ALLISON: I know we don't *have* to worry about you, but we do. We're your friends, Randy.

RANDY: I know you're my friends, it's just that . . .

ALLISON: You don't want to talk about it, right?

RANDY: Right. I mean, it's no big deal,

48

and I've worked it out already
anyway.

ALLISON: So then, why are you acting so
strangely?

RANDY: Look, Al, I'm really sorry about
the way I've been acting. I have
worked it out, it's just that I
haven't told my mother that I definitely want to go back yet.

ALLISON: What? Go back where?

Randy doesn't answer.

ALLISON: Go back to New York? Is that it?
Your mother wants to stay here,
and you want to go back?

RANDY: Yeah, that's it. Don't sound so
upset, Al. You knew that I was
going back at the end of the year.
I told you guys that from the
beginning.

ALLISON: Yes, you did. But I guess, I … I
mean … we … thought that you
really liked it here and were
going to stay.

RANDY: *I* never planned to stay, Al. My

mother has decided that her painting is going well and she might be offered a one-woman show next fall. She wants to stay, but I want to go back. I mean, it will be hard not living with her, but I can always live with my father.

ALLISON: Your mother will let you live with your father?

RANDY: Why not? She said she doesn't want me to be miserable.

ALLISON: I'm just surprised your mother would let you go, that's all.

RANDY: Well, she wants me to be happy.

ALLISON: That's true, I guess. I heard what happened in social studies today. Did you get into much trouble?

RANDY: *Please.* I had to write five hundred lines about not talking back in class. I can't handle all this discipline. Who'd you hear it from anyway, Sabs?

ALLISON: Yes.

RANDY: Well, there's nothing to worry about, okay? Listen, Al, I've got to

	get going if I'm going to be at the airport in time to meet Sheck.
ALLISON:	Oh, that's right. Sheck's coming in tonight. What will he do tomorrow?
RANDY:	Probably sleep all day, knowing him.
ALLISON:	Will we get to meet him?
RANDY:	Sure.
ALLISON:	Well, maybe you could bring him to Fitzie's after school tomorrow so everyone can meet him.
RANDY:	I don't know if that's quite his thing, Al. I mean, it's not exactly like New York, if you know what I mean. Sheck's used to a little more excitement.
ALLISON:	Oh. I guess that's probably true.
RANDY:	Well, maybe we'll go. Listen, I better get in gear here. I'll see you tomorrow, okay?
ALLISON:	Sure, Randy. I'll see you in home-room. Bye.
RANDY:	Ciao.

Allison calls Sabs.

ALLISON: Is Sabrina there, please?

SABRINA: Yeah, it's me.

ALLISON: Hi, it's Allison.

SABRINA: I know. What's up?

ALLISON: Well, I just talked to Randy.

SABRINA: You did! You mean she actually talked to you? Did she tell you about social studies? Did she get into trouble? What's going on with her, anyway? Is she all right? What did Mr. Hansen say to her, anyway? … Well?

ALLISON: Um … well, Randy did talk to me for a while, and I think I know why she's been acting so weird. I don't know what Mr. Hansen said, but she had to write something five hundred times in detention.

SABRINA: Al! What's wrong with her, anyway?

ALLISON: Well, she's going back to New York in June.

SABRINA: Oh, yeah! That's right. I forgot. I

wish she wasn't leaving. But why is that bothering her, if she always knew she was going back? Is her mother forcing her to go back against her will, or something? That's probably it — Randy really wants to stay, right?

ALLISON: Randy is definitely moving back there. And it bothers her now because. . .

Allison pauses.

SABRINA: Al, just tell me what's going on!

ALLISON: Well, Randy's mother wants to stay here, because —

SABRINA: That's great, so Randy can stay! But why is she going back, then?

ALLISON: Well, that's just it, Sabrina. Randy's mother wants to stay because her painting is going really well. Randy still wants to go back and live in New York.

SABRINA: She does? Why? I thought she liked it here.

ALLISON: Randy does like it here, Sabrina.

And I know she likes having all of us for friends. But I think that she just feels kind of out of place here. I don't think she feels like she fits in.

SABRINA: Of course she does. She's just different. But that's what makes her so much fun. I still don't get why she wants to move back.

ALLISON: Well, I think New York is safer for her.

SABRINA: What are you talking about? I hear even the sidewalks are dangerous in New York. How could it be safer there?

ALLISON: I don't mean like that, Sabrina. I mean that Randy is used to everything there, and she has a lot of friends. It's really different here, and she really stands out here.

SABRINA: But she's got us!

ALLISON: I know. And I think that we've got to be really understanding of her now. You know how she can get. I think that we just have to accept whatever she's going to do, and still be her friends.

SABRINA: Of course we'll still be her friends. It's ridiculous to think that we wouldn't. I just wish she wouldn't act like this. Friends are supposed to tell each other things.

ALLISON: Randy's just not like that, Sabrina.

SABRINA: You're probably right. So, we're just supposed to watch her go back to New York?

ALLISON: If it's what she wants to do.

SABRINA: I don't know about that. So what else did Randy tell you?

ALLISON: That was it. She had to leave for the airport.

SABRINA: Oh, that's right! Her friend, what's his name?

ALLISON: Sheck.

SABRINA: Sheck. That's a cool name. I wonder what he looks like. Do you think he'll be cute? I can't believe her best friend is a boy. Are we going to meet him, or what?

ALLISON: I have no idea what he looks like. But I do know Randy said she

might bring him to Fitzie's tomorrow after school so we could all
meet him.

SABRINA: I can't wait. Imagine a boy from
New York. I wonder what he's
like. Do you think he's anything
like Randy?

ALLISON: I don't know, Sabrina. Randy was
really excited that he was coming
to visit, though. She must have
missed him a lot. Maybe she'll
feel better about everything with
him here.

SABRINA: Hang on a second, Al.

Pause while Sabrina yells something.

SABRINA: Listen, Al, I'd better go. Sam's
yelling about clearing the table or
something. I know it's not my
turn, but you know how he is. He
can't do anything without making it into a big deal. What a pain.

ALLISON: Okay, Sabrina. So I'll see you
tomorrow in homeroom. And
don't worry about Randy. I'm

	sure she'll be better tomorrow.
SABRINA:	I'm sure she will, too. See ya tomorrow. Bye.
ALLISON:	Good night.

Forty-five minutes later, Sabrina calls Katie. Katie's older sister, Emily, answers the phone.

SABRINA:	Hi, is Katie there?
EMILY:	Just a second. Who's calling, please?
SABRINA:	It's Sabs.
EMILY:	Hold on.

Emily calls to Katie.

KATIE:	Hi, Sabs?
SABRINA:	Hi, Katie. What are you doing?
KATIE:	I'm working on that English paper.

Sabrina groans.

KATIE:	Sabrina Wells! Just because I like to get things done early, and you

	wait until the last minute, doesn't mean you should make fun of me or anything.
SABRINA:	I know. I was groaning because I don't even know what book I'm using yet, and you're probably finished already.
KATIE:	No, not yet. And if you need any help. . .
SABRINA:	I know, I know. You'll be happy to help me. I just can't seem to get everything done when it's supposed to be done. I think I have an organizational problem. I was reading something in the *Hollywood Star* about how all the biggest stars have people that actually organize their lives for them. So, don't you see, when I'm famous, I won't need to be organized. Somebody will do it for me.
KATIE:	That's not for a few years, though.
SABRINA:	You don't know that. I've read about all these people who were

	discovered in the supermarket or at the Laundromat — you know, in the most unglamorous places. It could happen any day.
KATIE:	When was the last time you were in a Laundromat?
SABRINA:	That's not important, Katie. I'm just saying it could happen anywhere, anytime. And then I won't need to worry about when my English paper's due and all that.
KATIE:	Well, you'll still have to do homework, I'm sure.
SABRINA:	What? When I'm a star?
KATIE:	Of course. At least until you're sixteen.

Sabrina groans again.

KATIE:	Hey, don't worry about it. You'll have somebody to tell you when papers are due and when you have tests and stuff.
SABRINA:	That's true. Well, listen, the reason I called is because I talked to Allison before, and she had talked

	to Randy.
KATIE:	Really. What's up with Randy? Did she get into a lot of trouble for what happened in social studies?
SABRINA:	Well, she got detention.
KATIE:	Detention!
SABRINA:	Come on, Katie. You know detention's not such a big deal, especially for Randy. Anyway, she only had to write some line five hundred times. Al said she didn't sound too torn up about the whole thing.
KATIE:	Well, it's good she didn't get into more trouble.
SABRINA:	Maybe. Listen, Randy is upset because she's moving back to New York!
KATIE:	Well, we knew that. What's she so upset about? She told us when we first met her that she was moving back in June.
SABRINA:	I kind of thought she'd be staying here. I mean, we're her friends, and I thought she was happy

here.

KATIE: Well, she's got lots more friends in New York, doesn't she? And her father's there and everything.

SABRINA: Yeah, that's true. But the problem is, is that Mrs. Zak—

KATIE: You mean Olivia, right?

SABRINA: Right, Olivia wants to stay here. Allison said that Randy said things are going really well for Olivia and she just doesn't want to go back to New York.

KATIE: Really? So why is Randy moving, then?

SABRINA: I guess she really wants to go back. Al said Randy was thinking about living with her father.

KATIE: What about Leighton?

SABRINA: I don't know. I think it would be pretty weird for your father to have a girlfriend. And it will be even worse if Randy's living with her dad. She'll have to see Leighton all the time.

KATIE: I know. What does her mother say to all this?

SABRINA: Well, Al said that Randy hadn't
            told Olivia anything yet.
KATIE: Do you think Mrs. Zak — I mean
            Olivia — will just let Randy go
            back to New York without her?
SABRINA: I don't know. I didn't ask Al that.
            I hadn't thought of it. I'm sure
            Olivia won't like that. She and
            Randy are like best friends or
            something. Ohmygosh!
            Speaking of best friends,
            Sheck is flying in tonight. Randy's
            picking him up at the airport
            right now!
KATIE: Oh, yeah. I forgot he was coming
            to visit. Is Randy excited?
SABRINA: Al said that Randy was really
            excited. You know, Sheck's visit
            will be good for Randy. But *I'm*
            really excited, too. Can you imag-
            ine? A real live boy from New
            York City! I wonder what he's
            like.
KATIE: Well, he's probably a lot like
            Randy, if they're best friends and
            all.

SABRINA: Yeah, but, Katie, I wonder if he's cute.

KATIE: Who knows? I guess we'll find out, won't we?

SABRINA: Allison did say that Randy was going to bring him to Fitzie's tomorrow after school. What the heck am I going to wear? I want to make a good impression on him. I want to look cool, you know?

KATIE: Don't worry about it, Sabs, I'm sure he'll like us. I mean, he is Randy's friend and all, right?

SABRINA: But what will I wear? I wish I could get something new.
See, I told you I needed
to get a bigger allowance.

KATIE: Calm down, Sabs. It's nothing to lose sleep over or anything.
Listen, I had better get back
to my English paper. You should probably start yours, too.

SABRINA: I know, I know. I will. Right after I pick out my clothes for tomorrow,
So I'll see you tomorrow?

KATIE: Right. Bye.
SABRINA: Bye.

Chapter Six

I was standing around the arrivals lounge at the airport, waiting for the plane from New York to land. My mother was outside waiting in the car. There were a lot of people everywhere, and I kept worrying that I'd miss him. I thought my eyes were going to pop out of my head, the way they were glued to the little white door the passengers were supposed to be coming through.

"Ran!" I suddenly heard a voice behind me say. I turned around and there was Sheck. I couldn't believe it. I almost didn't recognize him. He really had grown quite a few inches. We used to be the same height. He looked so ... different. I don't know if I'd quite agree with Samantha about him being a hunk, but he was definitely much cuter than I remembered. His curly black hair was longer, and I didn't remember his eyes being so green. He was wearing all black. Black was always our favorite color, even when we were little. He had on a black turtleneck with a zipper in the front, a black vest, faded black jeans, black shoes, and a big, long black overcoat. I have to admit, he did look great.

That was all I had a chance to think about, though, before Sheck hopped the rail and hugged me, lifting me off the ground. He spun me around a few times and then stopped.

"Ran, it's great to see ya!" he exclaimed. "You look great!"

So do you was what I wanted to say, but instead I just said, "I'm glad you're here, Sheck!"

"Hey, me too," he agreed. "But, I didn't think I'd ever get here. Hey, where's your mom?"

"She's out with the car," I said, remembering that my mother was waiting for us. Sheck grabbed my hand and we practically ran to the baggage claim area. Sheck talked nonstop the whole way out to the car. Then when he saw my mother he made her get out of the car so that he could give her a big hug. I don't think my mother and I managed to say two words during the entire trip back from the airport. But it was okay. There's something about Sheck that just puts everyone in a good mood.

"Hey, is this Acorn Falls?" Sheck asked as we drove down Main Street. "This reminds me of "The Andy Griffith Show" or something. Hey, don't blink, or you'll miss all of downtown, right?"

I giggled. That's exactly how I felt. It was good to have someone else thinking the same thing. Sabs, Katie, and Al never understood how small Acorn Falls seemed to me.

"Pardner," Sheck said in a terrible Western accent, "this is a real one-horse town."

Even my mother laughed at that one. "Well, I have to admit, I'm not used to cooking so much. Nobody delivers in this town."

"Ha!" I retorted. "You never cook, M. You know I do all the cooking."

Sheck laughed. He had been around our apartment enough in New York to remember my mother's very few, very weak attempts at cooking in the past. "No offense, Olivia, but I kind of believe Randy. Remember, I've experienced your chili."

My mother sniffed in mock hurt. "You survived, didn't you?"

We turned into Maple Street. "I can't get over the street names here, Ran," Sheck admitted. "When I wrote you, I thought your address was a total joke. But I guess it wasn't. And why don't you have a number on your house?"

"Well, Sheck, our name is on the mailbox," I said. "Why would we need numbers?"

Sheck snorted. Then we pulled into our driveway. For the first time all night, Sheck was speechless. Finally he found his voice. "This is where you live?" he asked, looking over at me. My mother had already started to get out of the car.

I nodded silently.

"Ran," he said slowly, "this is a *barn*, where cows and horses sleep. What's the deal here?"

I laughed. "Don't worry, Sheck. I won't get you up on your first morning to milk the cows. But after that, I make no promises."

Sheck gave me a worried look. "Are you for real?"

I jumped out and grabbed Sheck's suitcase from the backseat. He slid out of the car slowly. "What's the matter, Sheck? Afraid of a few farm animals?" I asked. It was really good to joke with someone about this little town. I was glad Sheck was here.

Sheck loved our house, I mean barn. I knew he would.

"Wild!" he exclaimed. "This reminds me of that big loft in SoHo that my sister got married in, remember, Ran?"

How could I forget? Sheck and I were really into cinema then, and we decided to videotape the whole thing. Sheck's sister, Zoe, threatened us with death if the tape didn't come out well, because she didn't hire anyone else as a back-up. I don't think it was quite what she had in mind. I remember crawling under the tables a lot to get some cool angles.

My mom showed Sheck around the barn. He went nuts over her paintings. "These are fantastic, incredible, superb, Olivia! Randy said you're going to be in a show soon. Is that true?"

Mom looked really pleased I had told Sheck about the show. "Yup, that's right. I'm a bona fide artist with recognition now. My paintings will be in a show for talented area artists this January in Minneapolis, and depending how that goes, I might do a one-woman show next fall."

"Rad! So you're going to come back here to do that?" Sheck asked.

My mother looked at me. I shook my head. I hadn't told Sheck anything about the New York versus Acorn Falls issue yet.

"Well, we haven't planned that far ahead yet," my mother said vaguely. "And the show is not for quite some time, anyway."

Sheck looked at me, and I shrugged.

"Listen," my mother continued. "I've got a bunch of letters to write, and a book that I bought last week, so you guys can watch television or whatever. Ran, don't forget to show Sheck where all the blankets are, and there's plenty of food in the fridge."

A few minutes later, when Sheck and I went into the kitchen to find some food, I could hear my mother playing Simon and Garfunkel on the cassette player in her room. Sheck started opening all the cupboards.

"What's all this stuff?" he asked, pointing to the oat bran, soy burger mix, and nuts in the cabinets. "Don't you have any real food here?"

I laughed. "M's been on a health food thing

since we first got out here. I have no idea why. All I can tell you is that I've been having midnight cravings for some greasy French fries smothered in gravy and an extra-thick strawberry shake, and there's no way my mother would ever keep those in the house," I admitted.

"Oh, yeah, from Neptune's?" Sheck asked. Neptune's is the diner we always went to in New York. They make the best shakes there. "When you come to New York for Christmas vacation, we'll go there as soon as you get off the plane."

I could see me sitting there with all my luggage, not even going home first. I laughed again. Sheck had definitely put me in a better mood.

"Hey, aren't you guys moving back to New York in June?" Sheck asked, his head buried in the refrigerator.

"*I* am," I said shortly. Sheck emerged holding a tub of tofu.

"What in the world is this?" he asked. "No, no, I don't want to know. So what about your mother?"

"Well, she may stay here," I admitted,

pulling out a big pot to make popcorn in.

"What!" Sheck exclaimed loudly, the tofu forgotten. "You're not going to stay, are you? You *have* to come back to New York. It's not the same without you."

"Shh!" I hissed. I didn't want my mother to hear this conversation. "I told you, I am going back home. I just haven't told my mother yet." I was secretly pleased that Sheck didn't think things were the same without me.

"Good," he said. Then he turned back to the refrigerator. "Don't you have anything to drink besides seltzer and bottled water?"

"Tea," I said, watching his face pucker up. Sheck lives on soda. He even drinks it for breakfast. It's incredible.

"I guess I'll have a glass of good old boring water. So when is the popcorn going to be ready?"

"In moments," I assured him. My mother always jokes that Sheck is like a human garbage disposal. He eats anything, but he has to eat all the time. It didn't look as if it was affecting him the wrong way, though. "Hey, let's get you settled and stuff."

"Settled?" Sheck asked, laughing. "You

sound like you belong in a Norman Rockwell painting or something."

"Jerk! You only know what those paintings look like," I retorted, pretending I was angry with him. "How would you know what the people in them sounded like?"

"I *know*," he said. "And you've become one of them. Watch out! Soon you'll be wearing gingham dresses and white aprons."

I threw the empty plastic seltzer bottle at him. He dodged it and ducked into the living room. "Please bring me my food and drink when you have prepared it," he called out over his shoulder.

I laughed. The day would never come when I waited on him, even if he was kidding. I've known him way too long for that.

But, in the end, I did. I brought an overflowing bowl of popcorn and two glasses of water into the living room. Sheck already had his shoes off and was stretched out on one of the sofas. "Please, sit here at my feet, so you can worship me and adore me," Sheck kidded me.

He couldn't dodge the popcorn I threw at him, but I sat down at the end of the couch, anyway. Chomping away, I hunted for the remote control. "Hey, maybe there's a stupid movie on," I said.

"What? You get cable here?" Sheck asked in surprise, sitting up. "I didn't think the signals went out this far."

I was kind of insulted, but I didn't say anything. Acorn Falls isn't that backward. We aren't in the middle of the wilderness or anything. I mean, Minneapolis is a major city, and it's only an hour or so away.

Alien was on. That was one of our all-time favorite movies. Sheck loves horror movies as much as my mother and I do. In fact, once we even did a report on horror movie victims for school. It was actually more of a list of *don't*s to follow in case you ever found yourself in a horror situation. Victims in horror movies are so stupid most of the time.

Sheck must have been thinking about the same thing I was, because he said, "Hey, Ran, remember — never split up." That was the number one thing on our list of "horror movie *don't*s."

"Right, and number two — don't investigate anything you don't need to," I said. I hate it when someone hears or sees something that definitely does not look normal, and walks toward it to get a better look. I mean, run away, have a little sense. It is a horror movie, after all.

"And number three — never run up," he added, laughing. He can't stand to watch someone who's being chased run *up* the stairs. What are they planning to do when they get to the roof — jump? It's always a mistake to run anywhere but down in those movies.

Sheck got up and started running around the living room. "This is my impression of the poor, innocent heroine being chased by the homicidal maniac," he said, grabbing one of the blankets I had brought out for him. "She's only wearing her nightgown, of course. And no shoes. She's running through the dark woods instead of toward the lit highway."

He wrapped the blanket around himself and proceeded to stumble into the furniture. "She should make sure to choose the noisiest route. You know, with a lot of dead leaves and dry branches, so the maniac knows which way she's going." Suddenly Sheck let out a small gasp, tripped over his own foot, and fell down, looking behind him. "It's very important to fall. And when she falls, she has to make sure that she looks back so she gets a really good look at the maniac before he chops her head off with his chain saw."

I was laughing hysterically by this time. But it was so true. The people in these movies really did act like that. Sheck is totally crazy. Boy, did I miss him. I mean, my friends here are fun and all, but they aren't crazy — not the way Sheck is.

I stood up and said, "Well, if I'm the lucky one chosen to survive, what should I do after I kill the maniac?" I grabbed a pillow and hit Sheck over the head with it. "Yes, I know I have killed the indestructible homicidal maniac with this lethal pillow, because he looks dead, right?" I threw the pillow over my shoulder and sat down, next to Sheck, and put my face in my hands. "So it's very important that I sit with my back to the immortal maniac, so that when he gets his second wind, I'm within easy reach."

Sheck pretended to stab me in the back. "Hey, Ran," he said softly, helping me get back up on the couch. "It really is good to see you again, seriously. I really missed you."

He tossed me a blanket and grabbed the bowl of popcorn off the table. "And I'm really glad you're coming back to New York, after all. It will be good for you to get back. I mean, what do you do for fun here? Do you go to the movies and then out for an ice cream soda afterward? Or maybe the big Friday night football game? Give me a break."

"I guess that's what I do," I said quietly, watching the movie. But I felt kind of bad agreeing with Sheck about Acorn Falls. After all, I didn't hate it here, and Sheck's description made it sound awful. I decided Sheck really didn't know what he was talking about. "It's really not all that bad, Sheck," I added.

Sheck gave me a look of shock. "What are you talking about, Randy?" he asked. "This place is backward."

"No, it's not," I disagreed. "It's just different."

"Come on, Ran," Sheck replied disbelievingly. "I faintly remember a letter 'someone' wrote me in September. Let me see if I can remember the words." He paused for a moment.

"Sheck," I began, trying to stop him. But there was no stopping Sheck when he got going.

"'Dear Sheck, this place is incredible,'" he continued. "'Minnesota is full of preppies. I've never seen so many polo shirts in my life. You would think I came here from another planet the way everyone stares at me. I think it might be my clothes, but there's no way I would ever wear a turtleneck as my main article of clothing.'" He stopped and grinned at me. "Should I go on?"

I couldn't believe it! Those were almost my exact words. Sheck must have read that letter more than once.

"Sheck!" I exclaimed. "That was early in the school year. It's gotten a lot better since I started hanging out with Sabs, Katie, and Allison. It's really not so bad now."

Sheck looked unconvinced. "Right," he replied. Then he proceeded to stuff an entire handful of popcorn in his mouth. "Hey, this is my favorite part. That alien is totally cool," he commented, changing the subject.

After the movie was over, I got Sheck all "settled" on the long couch. He looked perfectly comfortable, and I could have sworn he was snoring by the time I finished brushing my teeth.

Climbing the stairs to my room, I thought about what Sheck had said. I think Acorn Falls is a little slow, but I didn't like hearing someone else talk about it. I mean, I live here, he doesn't. So how could he know what it's really like? He hadn't even been here the entire day and already he was totally ranking on the place. I mean, it might not be New York, but Acorn Falls wasn't nearly as bad as Sheck seemed to think it was.

Chapter Seven

Before I left for school the next morning, I checked on Sheck. He was sprawled all over the couch and snoring so loudly that I was glad we didn't live in an apartment and the neighbors could hear. Sheck hates mornings even more than I do. Back in New York, he hardly ever got to school until after first period was over.

I left him a note on the kitchen table, telling him to meet me at Fitzie's after school. I drew a little map at the bottom of the paper so he could find his way, but I really wasn't worried. Knowing Sheck, he'd probably cruise around on his skateboard for a while, checking everything out. In a way, he's kind of like Sabrina. He always wants to know what's going on.

I was feeling pretty good this morning. Life had been so confusing ever since M told me she wanted to stay in Acorn Falls. But now that I'd made the decision to go back to New York at the end of the school year, everything could go back to normal.

I saw Sabs at her locker before first period, but she was hunting for her math homework and didn't have time to talk. I wondered if Allison had told her about my decision, but thought I'd better wait until homeroom to bring it up.

When I got to homeroom, Allison, Katie, and Sabs were standing by my desk, looking serious and talking really quietly. I didn't have to be a psychic like Allison to tell that something was up.

"Randy?" Sabs said, sounding kind of nervous. She was biting her lip and looked like she was having trouble thinking of what to say. Sabs, who never runs out of things to say? What was going on here?

"Allison told us that you ... um ... decided to go back to New York when school's over next year. I mean, we sort of knew you wanted to do that, but I guess we all kind of hoped ... Anyway, you'll probably think it's kind of corny, but we just wanted you to know that whatever you end up doing, we'll always be your friends."

She was right. It *was* pretty corny. But why did I have this lump in my throat? Even though I'd never admit it, I was kind of glad she'd said that. I looked at Allison. I knew she'd been the one to tell Katie and Sabs not to try and talk me into staying. Someday I'm going to have to talk to her about the way she reads my mind.

"Hey, do you guys want to go to Fitzie's after school today?" I asked them, changing the subject. "I'm sure Sheck could really get into a strawberry sundae."

"Oh, wow! I almost forgot about Sheck! Where is he? Has he changed a lot? What does he look like?" Sabrina was practically lying on my desk, she was so curious.

"Relax, Sabs! He'll be at Fitzie's after school. You can see what he looks like for yourself."

The bell rang just then, and all the kids rushed to their seats before Ms. Staats started screaming.

I was really looking forward to spending the afternoon with Sheck, so, naturally, the day dragged on. The only good part of the day was lunch. Right after lunch, I had a pop quiz in science class, but since science is my best subject, I didn't have any problem with it. In social studies, the Rug glared at me when I first came in, but I stared right back, and eventually he decided to ignore me, which suited me just fine.

Finally, eighth period was over. I could hardly wait to see Sheck again. The four of us met at my locker and ran out of the school toward Fitzie's. When we got there, Stacy the Great and her friends were sitting in the booth by the jukebox, giggling.

We sat down in a booth on the other side and ordered. I made sure I could see the door from where I was sitting, so I'd see Sheck as soon as he got there. Sabs was in the middle of a really complicated story about what had happened to Kristin, her favorite cousin, when she went on a blind date. Then Sheck walked in with a skateboard tucked under his arm.

By now Fitzie's was really busy, and it took him a minute to find me. When he did, he nodded, then started pushing through the crowd to get to our booth.

"Randy! Why didn't you tell us he was

such a hunk?" asked Sabrina with this really dreamy look in her eyes. It's the same look she gets when she's thinking about her latest crush, but she was looking at Sheck!

"Have you flipped your lid, Sabs? Sheck isn't a hunk, he's just ... Sheck!" I might as well have been talking to a brick wall. Sabrina was practically drooling all over the table. I turned back toward Sheck. I had to admit, he did look pretty good. He had on a really old pair of jeans with holes in the knees, a black mock-turtleneck shirt, and a great leather jacket. I had helped him pick out the jacket in New York.

Sabrina wasn't the only one who had noticed Sheck. As he walked toward us, all the girls he passed stopped talking and followed him with their eyes. Even Stacy the Great stopped giggling over whatever Jason McKee had just said to her, and stared. She recovered quickly, stood up, and flashed him this big smile. Then she flipped her long, blond hair over her shoulder and started batting her eyelashes at him. I had to grit my teeth to keep from throwing up.

The worst part was that Sheck smiled right

back! And then he started walking toward her! He was walking weird, too, kind of the way Sabs's brother Sam does when he's trying to impress some girl. I couldn't believe he was showing off for a brainless bingo head like Stacy. Then he started talking to her, and she proceeded to introduce her clones. All of them were smiling and laughing and making complete idiots out of themselves!

Sheck was supposed to be visiting me! Why was he wasting his time on Stacy Hansen? What was going on here? I was so mad I felt like there was smoke coming out my ears.

I felt a hand on my arm and turned to see Allison looking at me. "Don't worry, Randy," she said quietly. "It won't take him long to figure out what Stacy's really like."

"Who's worried?" I said. "It's not like I own him or anything."

"I just don't want you to be jealous," Allison went on.

"Me? Jealous? Be real, Allison! Sheck and I are just friends!" My voice was squeaking for some reason, so I took a sip of water to soothe my throat.

"Hey, Zak," Sheck said, coming up and

sliding into the booth next to us. I grunted at him, then went back to eating my banana split. Sheck shrugged, then looked over at my friends.

"Hi, I'm Sheck."

"Hi, Sheck. I'm Sabrina, and this is Katie, and that's Allison. Randy's told us a lot about you." Sabs was talking really fast, the way she always does when she's excited.

Sheck looked at me and winked. "Yeah, Randy's told me all about you guys, too."

I looked at Sheck quickly. What was he talking about? I had hardly told him anything about my friends in Acorn Falls. Sheck's eyes lit up, like they used to when he was trying to get away with something at school.

"So what do you think of Acorn Falls?" Katie asked.

Sheck winked at me again. "It sure is different. Very ... peaceful," he said.

Why didn't he just come right out and say he thought it was boring? What was he doing?

"Yeah, living in New York must be really exciting. I've always wanted to go there." Sabrina sighed. "After L.A., no, maybe before. Oh, I don't know." Sabs giggled. She does that a lot — contradicts herself and babbles.

But Sheck wasn't even paying attention to Sabs anymore. He was looking out into the crowd of kids in Fitzie's, and for a moment I had no idea why. Then Stacy the Great walked up to our table.

"Hi, Sheck. My friends and I are leaving now, and I just wanted to come over and say good-bye." Somehow Stacy managed to single Sheck out, completely ignoring the fact that he was sitting with Al, Katie, Sabs, and me. Katie rolled her eyes, Sabs stuck her finger in her mouth, pretending to throw up, and Al stared out the window, watching a few flakes of snow fall. My eyes were glued to Sheck.

"And don't forget about my party Friday night," Stacy went on, batting her eyelashes some more.

"Bye, Stacy," Sheck said, grinning. "I'd love to come to your party, but I'm staying with a friend, and it kind of depends on what she wants to do." Then he turned and looked at me. I was about to tell Stacy that I would never be caught dead at her stupid party when Sabrina suddenly cut in.

"I don't think Randy has any plans for

Friday night, Sheck. In fact, none of us do. We'd love to bring Sheck to your party, Stacy," she continued, oblivious to our shocked expressions. "Everybody's heard about it. We can't let Sheck go home to New York City without showing him how we party in Acorn Falls, you know."

Katie, Al, and I were all staring at Sabrina. Did she know what she was doing? She had just invited all of us to Stacy's party — and there was no way Stacy could get out of it with Sheck sitting there listening to the whole thing! I couldn't believe it!

"Awesome!" said Sheck, grinning even wider than before. "We'll bring a couple of our tapes, Zak. That'll blow the roof off the place!"

"I wouldn't miss this for the whole world!" Sabs gushed. "What time does the party start, again, Stacy?"

Stacy looked as though she'd been slapped. Her face was really pale and there were bright red spots on her cheeks. She was trapped! "S-s-seven o'clock," she stuttered, then turned around and practically ran back to her table.

"See you then!" Sabrina sang after her, then collapsed into laughter over her brownie sundae.

Katie was almost on the floor, she was laughing so hard, and even Allison was giggling.

"Way to go, Sabs!" Katie gasped finally, wiping tears from her eyes. "I wish I had a picture of her face when she realized ..." and Katie dissolved into hysterics again.

"Yeah, but just think about how she'll act when we show up on her doorstep on Friday night!" Sabrina said. Even I started to laugh, thinking about how angry it was going to make Stacy the Great when the four of us came walking into her party with Sheck.

"Hey, Ran," Sheck said, looking kind of confused at all of the laughter. I suddenly realized that he had no clue that he'd helped Sabs ruin Stacy's whole week! "I promised your mother we would be home pretty early, and there's too much snow to skateboard, so maybe we should get going, huh?"

I looked out the window to see that almost half an inch of snow was on the ground already. I picked up my bag and jacket, said good-bye to Allison, Katie, and Sabs, then headed home with Sheck.

"Whew!" Sheck exclaimed as soon as we walked out of Fitzie's. "The snow sure comes down fast out here in the sticks! If we'd stayed much longer, we might have been snowed in at Fitzie's for Thanksgiving! The strawberry sundaes were pretty good, but I felt like I was in a time warp or something."

"Well, it's a little old-fashioned," I said slowly. *But so what*, I thought. Just because it wasn't the most state-of-the-art place didn't mean it wasn't fun.

"*A little?*" Sheck was practically having a heart attack on the spot. "Randy, you've been away from New York too long. We've got to get you back into the real world."

"You seemed to think Stacy Hansen was pretty cool," I replied with a frown.

"Who? Oh, yeah, the blond who's having the party on Friday." Sheck waved his hand in the air as if he were brushing Stacy aside. "I guess we'll have to go to her party, since your friend Sabrina said we would." He laughed. "Your friends looked kind of excited about it."

I didn't say anything. There was something about Sheck's tone of voice that was really getting to me. For some reason I started thinking about going ice-skating with Katie, and how much fun we'd had. I thought about all the tricks we'd played on Sabs's brothers when we'd had sleepovers at her house. Then I thought about Allison and the way she always seemed to know what I was feeling before I really knew myself. There was nobody like them back in New York. I was definitely starting to get pretty annoyed with Sheck.

"Hey! While I was checking out the town this afternoon, I came up with a really great idea for a horror flick about all these gory deaths in a quiet little midwestern suburb," Sheck said. "We could call it *The Attack of the Killer Boredom Monster*, and you and I could be the stars." Sheck was all wrapped up in his movie idea. He didn't even notice I was upset. "We wouldn't even have to build a set for it or anything. All we would need is this really backward town. Acorn Falls is perfect."

I was starting to get mad. Here was Sheck, in town for less than twenty-four hours, and he thought he had the right to just rank all over it like this? He didn't know what he was talking about!

Sheck waved his hand around again. "If you want, we can even let your friends be in it. Sabrina could be the first victim. A redhead always gets people's attention. And Katie — she'd have to die early, too. The audience loves those all-American types. And that other girl — Alice? — what's the story with her? Is she Indian or something?"

I gritted my teeth. "Her name is Allison Cloud and, yes, she is one hundred percent Chippewa."

"Great! I'll have to think of a good way to use that in the plot," Sheck went on.

"I bet the hero falls in love with Stacy Hansen," I muttered to myself, kicking at the snow.

"We could even use that blond who's having the party on Friday," Sheck said. "Maybe she and the hero could have this thing going, and he could rescue her from the monster at the last minute."

"Oh, Sheck, please!" I yelled. "That has got to be the worst idea I've ever heard! Acorn Falls would be a terrible place for a horror movie."

"Yeah, you're right. I feel really sorry for you, having to stay here till the school year's over."

I stopped walking and turned to face him. "That's not what I meant. Allison, Katie, and Sabs — they're my *friends*. We have a lot of fun together and —"

"Ran! Randy! Cool it!" Sheck said quickly. "Look, I know you're just trying to make the best of all this. But Acorn Falls, Minnesota, is just not you, and you know it. You're a New Yorker. You belong in the city. One week back with us and you'll forget that you were ever out here. Now come on, let's get going. I'm hungry."

Sheck started off toward my house, breaking a path through the layer of snow that kept getting thicker and thicker. I stomped after him, thinking furiously about what he had said. Yes, I wanted to go back to New York. But I didn't want to forget about Acorn Falls! I had friends here, good friends. I started thinking about all the things Allison, Katie, Sabrina, and I had planned for the rest of the year, and I realized it wasn't going to be easy to leave them. I hadn't thought about it before, but when I left for New York, I was really going to miss Acorn Falls, Minnesota.

Chapter Eight

I woke up early on Thanksgiving morning.
The storm had turned into a blizzard, and we'd
had a snow day on Wednesday. The snow had
finally stopped Wednesday night. It was piled up
in huge drifts everywhere. It was incredible. I
don't think I'd ever seen that much snow before.
It never snowed like this in New York City, that
was for sure.

I didn't feel like getting out of bed. It was so
nice to lie there all warm, wrapped up in my
quilt, looking outside at all the snow. The sun was
streaming through my dormer window, and I felt
very cozy. There was something really peaceful
about the whole thing. I wondered why Sheck
couldn't seem to appreciate the nice things about
Acorn Falls. He definitely hadn't spent enough
time here to know.

I could hear my mother downstairs in the
kitchen. Pots and pans were rattling. I thought

she had been kidding when she said she was going to make a big Thanksgiving dinner. But I could smell the turkey cooking, and it smelled delicious.

I rolled over and got up. I couldn't stay in bed on a day like this. It was just too beautiful out. It's funny, I never really thought about the weather much before. Back home I didn't spend much time outside, except for skateboarding. Here in Acorn Falls everyone stayed outside all the time. They went ice-skating, hiking, and everything. Today Sheck and I were supposed to go tobogganing at Bunn Hill with Sabs, Katie, and Allison. I'd never been tobogganing before — sledding on a little slope in Central Park wasn't the same. I thought it might be fun. Sabs had said it was a real big toboggan, big enough for all of us. It was going to be good to get out of the house after being cooped up the day before because of the blizzard. At least my mother had stocked up on a good supply of horror movie tapes.

I pulled a sweatshirt and jeans on over my long johns, and a pair of socks, and headed downstairs.

"Everything smells great, M," I said, kissing her on the cheek. She looked up, startled.

"What's that for, Ran?" she asked. She was covered with flour and her hands were coated with pumpkin goop. She had told me she wanted to make a pumpkin pie from scratch, but I didn't expect her to use a real pumpkin.

"I'm just happy, is that a crime?" I asked her, opening the oven to sniff the turkey.

"Oh, no," said M, "but you haven't been too happy lately, have you?"

I kind of ignored her because I didn't want to get into the whole thing again. "I'm going to wake up Sheck," I said, taking the orange juice out of the refrigerator. "That boy would sleep his life away if we let him." I poured a glass and headed into the living room.

Sheck was sleeping peacefully on the couch. I grinned wickedly. This was going to be good. I went over to the television and cranked the volume up as high as it would go, and then I turned the TV on. The sound came blaring out. Sheck jumped up and began looking around wildly. It was really funny. Then he saw me standing there and gave me a dirty look.

"What are you doing, Zak? It's the middle of the night," he said. "Go away and let me sleep."

I laughed and sat down at the end of the couch,

pushing his feet out of my way. "Happy Thanksgiving to you, too," I said, nudging him. "Come on, get up. The Thanksgiving parade is starting soon. I don't want to miss any of it."

I turned the volume down and found the right channel. The Macy's Thanksgiving Day parade was just starting — live from New York. I was so excited. This was the first year since I could remember that I hadn't been there in person. My father always took me to Macy's to sit in the bleachers and watch. It was great, no matter how cold it was. At least I could still watch it on television. I was secretly afraid they wouldn't show it in Minnesota.

Sometimes it's hard for me when I'm reminded of home. Like the parade. I begin to think about everything I left behind and how much I miss everyone in New York. Being with Sheck and watching the parade made me feel really ... homesick. Why didn't my mother want to go back home?

"Hey," Sheck said suddenly, reaching out to grab my orange juice. "What smells so good?"

I laughed. "My mom's making a big Thanksgiving dinner," I said. "Can you believe it?"

"No, not after her chili," he retorted, and then smiled. "It smells really good, though. I guess your mother has changed since she moved to the boondocks."

"Hey, it's not so bad here, Sheck. So stop picking on everything," I said, surprising myself. It might be okay for me to rank on Acorn Falls, but it was definitely not okay for Sheck to. I mean, he didn't even live here.

Sheck raised his eyebrow at me and then shrugged. "Whatever you say," he said.

It felt really strange to be watching the Thanksgiving parade on television. But I think the television coverage was almost better than being there. I mean, when I went to the parade everyone performed with their backs to the bleachers because they wanted to face the cameras. Now, on television, I could actually see all their faces and everything.

"Hey, don't forget we're going out later," I reminded Sheck.

"Oh, yeah," he replied. "We're going tobogganing, aren't we? I guess that's the big fun out here in the country, huh?"

I threw a pillow at him. "Cut it out, Sheck! You don't have to go if you don't want to! I wish you'd stop complaining just because things here are different."

I couldn't believe those words had just left my lips. I mean, that was exactly what my mother had been telling me all along. All she wanted was for me to give Acorn Falls a fair chance and to stop dwelling on the past. Maybe my Chinese fortune cookie fortune was right. Maybe change does make the world go around. I'd have to think about that.

Sheck was quiet for a little while. Then he apologized. "I'm sorry, Randy. I guess I have been a little hard on Acorn Falls. But it's so different from New York. It's kind of hard to see you here. I didn't mean what I said about going tobogganing. I think it'll be fun." Then he grinned. "Why do they call it a toboggan anyway?"

I laughed. I couldn't stay mad at Sheck for long. He's always been able to make me laugh. We watched the rest of the parade together, and my mother came in later to watch Santa Claus make his way to Thirty-fourth Street. Then Sheck and I set the table. My mother made us get dressed and we all ate the huge dinner she had prepared. It was a lot of fun. And the pumpkin pie was incredible.

"I'm totally stuffed, Olivia," Sheck said, tipping back in his chair. "That was great. But I don't think I'll ever eat again."

"I'll definitely never eat again," I moaned. "I mean it. I'm going to explode right now."

"Well, maybe you should go outside or something, so you won't mess up the house," my mother joked. "It would be such a terrible mess to clean up."

"Really, Ran," Sheck agreed. "The least you could do is implode if you have to do anything."

I laughed. "Listen, Sheck, we probably should get going soon. I told Sabs we'd get to her house around two-thirty."

My mother looked at the mess on the table, and then at us. "Hey, don't worry about the mess," she reassured us. "I think I'll visit Marybeth. She invited me for coffee." Marybeth is my friend Spike's mother. Spike's in the ninth grade and plays lead guitar for Wide Awake, a high school band. He lives down the street from us, and we've been friends since I moved here. His parents got divorced seven years ago. My mother and his mother are pretty good friends, actually.

"I'll clean it up when I get back," my mother continued. "You guys should put some warmer clothes on and get moving if you plan to be on time."

Sheck and I rushed around trying to get ready. "What do you wear tobogganing, anyway?" he kept shouting from downstairs.

Finally we were ready to go. I couldn't believe

Sheck. He was wearing jeans, a pair of work boots, one of my mother's old Swiss sweaters, and a turtleneck. He looked so preppie, I couldn't help laughing.

"What?" he demanded. "What's the problem?"

I laughed harder. "If only everyone back home could see the preppie you've become —"

"Shut up, Zak," he retorted, laughing. "You're just jealous. You probably wanted to wear this sweater."

"Right," I agreed. I, of course, was wearing all black — black jeans, thick black sweater, and lace-up black boots with rubber-soled treads. I even had black mittens. "Come on, let's go."

Sabs was still getting ready when we got to her house. Sheck and I sat in her big kitchen waiting for her to finish dressing. Sabs's brothers kept running in and out. Mrs. Wells offered us some pie, but I was much too full to even think about food. Sheck, garbage disposal that he is, had a huge piece of apple pie — with ice cream. I couldn't believe him. How could he eat again?

Finally Sabs came downstairs wearing an old pair of jeans, a big white hat, white mittens, and a large blue sweater with people skating on it. She looked really cute.

While we were waiting for Sabs to get her

toboggan out of the garage, Sheck turned to me and said, "You know, Sabrina seems like a really nice girl. She's just different from anyone I've ever met. And her mother makes great apple pie."

"We're meeting Katie and Al there, right?" Sabs asked, as she emerged from the garage, dragging the huge toboggan behind her.

The toboggan had a really long rope attached to the front, and not a lot of snow had been plowed yet, probably because it was a holiday, so it was really easy to pull it to Bunn Hill. Sheck made us both hop on, and he ran wildly down the sidewalk pulling us behind him. Then the sidewalk sloped downhill, and the toboggan started going faster than Sheck was running. The sled knocked into him, and he fell on top of us. The sled picked up more and more speed as we zoomed down the hill. I didn't think we'd arrive alive at Bunn Hill the way things were going. But luckily we hit a very large snowbank and came to a stop. We all got faces full of snow, though. Sheck and Sabrina looked pretty funny with snowy eyebrows.

I didn't know what to expect at Bunn Hill, so I was surprised by what I saw. It seemed as if the whole town was there. I was relieved to find

Allison and Katie right away, because there were so many people.

The five of us proceeded to drag the toboggan to the top of Bunn Hill. It was at least a fifteen-minute climb.

"They should put in ski lifts or something," Sheck complained on the way up. "Can I hail a taxi from here?"

At last we got to the top and got into a line to sled down.

"Should we do an easier trail or that one with the jump?" Sabs asked Katie right before it was our turn.

Trail with a jump? I couldn't believe there was more than one trail. Sledding was really big in Acorn Falls — almost as big as skiing. I didn't say anything, but I hoped we'd try an easy trail first. Somehow, sledding in Central Park seemed much safer than this hill. I could tell Sheck was a little nervous, too.

"Let's go down the one with the jump," Al said, surprising me. I turned to her, and she just smiled. "I love to sled" was all she said.

Sabs climbed in the front, with Allison right behind her. Sheck and I were third and fourth, and Katie was at the rear. Katie gave us a big push before she jumped on.

"You mean Sabs is steering?" I asked no one in particular. Already we were picking up speed. I could feel the wind burning my cheeks, so I tried to lean into the turns the way Sabs had told us to. Suddenly we went around this really sharp turn, and the next thing I knew, we were flying. It was totally wild. Sheck let out his really loud war whoop, and we hit the ground. We must have had a lot of height on that jump. I didn't think I'd be able to sit down for a week.

Before I knew it, Sabs and Allison were trying to stop the toboggan. They couldn't coordinate the whole thing and ended up tipping us over instead of just stopping.

"That was wild!" I exclaimed as I got up out of the snowbank where we'd landed. "That was great!" I couldn't wait to do it again.

"Can we do it again?" Sheck asked when he'd finished brushing the snow off his sweater. "That was really cool!"

Sabs and Katie just grinned. Al already had the sled by the rope and was heading back up the hill with it. We raced after her and all jumped on it. She stopped short and dug her heels in the snow to keep from sliding back down. "Not fair, you guys," she said, smiling. "You need a horse for this."

"No," Sheck disagreed. He jumped off the sled and took the rope from Allison. "You just need a manly man."

I snorted and everyone else laughed. Allison jumped on the sled, and we watched Sheck struggle. Finally he gave up and let go. We went sliding back down to the bottom and tipped over again. When I was able to stand up, I saw Sheck laughing. We all grabbed some snowballs and took off after him. I don't think he was too happy with all that cold snow down his back, but he deserved it. Then he vowed revenge.

"You're not a he-man," I teased him. He picked me up and tossed me into the snow. I just lay there for a second, trying to get my breath back. Then Sheck held out his hand and pulled me up. The light was fading a little, and it was funny because Sheck just sort of stood there staring at me, while the other three girls carted the toboggan up the hill. Then he brushed some snow out of my hair and touched my cheek for a split second with his glove.

Suddenly Sheck turned, made a few snowballs, and ran after my friends. I just stood there in the snow with this silly grin plastered across my face. I felt so ... so ... happy all of a sudden. Was it possible that I had a crush on Sheck? That thought made me smile even more, it seemed so ridiculous. I was going to have to talk to Sabs about this. She'd probably read about it in at least one of her magazines. Best friends and boyfriends, or something like that.

The five of us tobogganed until dark. By that time a lot of the other tobogganers had left. Everything seemed so peaceful, and the snow looked really pretty. I couldn't remember the last time I'd had such a good time. We all kept laughing over the silliest things. It was a wonderful time even though I was so cold I could hardly feel my toes or my fingers anymore.

Then we all went back to Sabs's house. Mrs. Wells had huge amounts of hot chocolate and cookies waiting for us. I was on my fourth cookie when Sheck said, "I thought you were never eating again."

"I changed my mind," I retorted and reached for another cookie.

"It's a woman's prerogative," Sabs said smugly. She loves quoting her magazines whenever she can.

Katie laughed. "Whatever that means, Sabs," she said. "Sabs changes her mind a lot," Katie informed Sheck.

"That's not true," Sabs replied. "But I do think

it's mysterious and unpredictable to change your mind all the time."

"That's true," Al agreed, sipping her hot chocolate. "And you are very unpredictable, Sabrina."

"My toes are cold," I complained. Sheck grabbed my feet and started rubbing my toes to warm them up.

"Better?" he asked, not looking up.

I couldn't even manage an answer. Luckily I didn't have to. Sabs's twin brother, Sam, and his best friends, Nick Robbins and Jason McKee, burst into the kitchen.

"I hope you didn't eat all the cookies, Sabs," Sam said as he took off his down jacket and scarf. Nick and Jason did the same.

"Mom made five dozen cookies, Sam," Sabs answered him.

"Right," Sam agreed. "So I hope you didn't eat all of them."

"Sam!" Sabs practically screamed and threw a dish towel at him. He ducked, and it hit Nick in the face. Sabs started to blush. Sam and Jason started laughing hysterically.

"Sorry," Sabs mumbled, not looking at Nick. It must be kind of weird for her to know that Nick likes her, and he's always at their house because he's Sam's best friend.

Anyway, they all sat down with us and had hot chocolate and cookies. Soon all the guys started talking about football with Sheck. Just because we're girls, boys never think we can carry on a conversation about football. It doesn't matter that I was the one who taught Sheck all the rules when we were in the fourth grade.

I couldn't believe it was almost eight o'clock when Mr. Wells came into the kitchen and mentioned that it was getting late. The time had just flown by. I was really glad all my friends were getting along so well. I could tell Sheck was having a good time, and he looked more unhappy about leaving than I did.

I kept thinking about how great Katie, Sabs, and Al are. Next to Sheck, they really were my best friends in the whole world. It was funny, because New York and my life there suddenly began to seem very far away.

Chapter Nine

It was Friday night and almost time for Stacy's big party. Thanksgiving vacation had just flown by. Sheck was supposed to go back to New York in two days. He wanted me to go with him, but of course I couldn't do that. No matter what happened, I had to stay until school was over in the spring.

"What do I wear to a party in Acorn Falls?" Sheck yelled from downstairs.

"How should I know?" I screamed back.

"You live here," he said. "Don't tell me this is the first party you've gone to since you've been here."

I laughed. "Of course not," I answered as I clattered down the stairs. "Listen, just wear whatever you want."

Sheck made an exaggerated face at me and turned back toward his suitcase.

"Listen, why don't you just hurry up and jump in the shower?" I added. "We're going to be late."

"Story of my life," Sheck retorted, laughing. He picked up his whole suitcase and carried it into the bathroom with him. "Randy," he said right before he shut the bathroom door, "you cannot rush fashion. Please remember that in the future."

I laughed and headed toward my mother's studio. I hadn't had much of a chance to talk to her alone since Sheck came to visit. I had spent Friday at the mall with Katie, Allison, Sabs, and Sheck, but I had done a lot of thinking in the past week. If my mother had asked me on Monday or Tuesday about what I wanted to do, I definitely would have told her that I couldn't stay in Acorn Falls. But, after all the fun we'd had the last few days, I really didn't want to leave. I mean, Sheck would always be my best friend. But that didn't mean that the friendships I had with Sabs, Katie, and Al weren't important. They were just different. Maybe because they were girls, and I had never had a girl for a best friend before.

And then I thought about my mother. I knew she wanted to stay here, and for the first time she was accomplishing something by herself, without any help from my father. I think it's important to her. I didn't think it was fair for me to make her leave.

My mother was mixing paints when I pulled up a stool next to her. "Mom, can I talk to you?" I asked.

"What's up, Ran?" my mother asked, putting her paintbrush down. She looked very serious, as if she already knew what I wanted to talk about.

"Well," I began, picking up a paintbrush and stroking the bristles, "I just wanted to tell you that if you want to stay longer in Acorn Falls... well... it's fine with me."

My mother smiled. It was a huge smile. I thought her face wouldn't be able to contain it, it was so big. "It is?" she asked.

I just nodded. I don't know why, but I felt as if I was about to cry. I can't remember the last time I cried. I was glad my mother was so happy. She reached over and gave me a big hug, and pushed the hair off my face.

"I'm so glad!" she exclaimed. "After our conversation last Friday, I really didn't think you wanted to stay here. But, you know, I think we are going to be really happy here. It's good to get away from New York and live somewhere different for a while."

I could only nod again. Maybe she was right. I had spent my whole life in New York City. A change might be good for me.

"Randy! I'm out of the shower!" Sheck yelled from the other room. I rolled my eyes at my mother.

"You know," I confided in her, "he doesn't know how to talk in a normal tone. He yells all the time."

"Yes, I know," my mother agreed. "But I don't think you mind it so much."

Startled, I looked at her. She just smiled at me with this knowing look on her face. "You better go get in the shower. You don't want to be late for the party, do you?"

I gave my mother another hug and turned to find Sheck.

Half an hour later, we were both ready to go. Sheck had decided to wear a white T-shirt, an over-sized black blazer, black-and-white-checked pleat-ed pants, and black shoes. I have to admit, he looked really good. I was wearing a funky red sleeveless dress with a long skirt and a scoop neck. I wore a black cropped jacket of my mother's over it. I was also wearing black flats with very pointy toes.

I thought I looked okay, but not great, so I didn't understand why Sheck whistled so much when I came downstairs. My mother came out of her studio at the commotion. She said that I looked really nice, too. Just then the doorbell rang. It was Sabrina.

"Hey, Ran," she said as I opened the door. "You guys look terrific!" Her eyes widened at the sight of Sheck behind me. "I love your dress, Randy."

"Thanks." I smiled.

"Hi, Mrs. Zak — I mean Olivia," Sabs added. "We better get going, I can hear Luke gunning the engine outside." Luke is one of Sabs's brothers. He just got his license over the summer, and he ends up driving her around a lot. He always acts as if it's a total pain to drive us places, but secretly I think he likes it. "Katie and Al are waiting in the car," Sabs added.

Sheck and I kissed my mother good-bye, grabbed our jackets, and followed Sabrina outside. "Phone me if you need a ride home!" my mother called after us.

Luke was driving the family station wagon. It was a good thing, too. The car was packed. Sabs and Allison were sitting in the front seat. Sam, Katie, Nick, and Jason were sitting behind the driver's seat. I really didn't know where Sheck and I were going to sit. Luckily, Jason and Sam jumped into the very back, and Katie and Nick slid over to make room for us.

We all made a lot of noise, and Luke had to keep

telling us to quiet down. Luke has these rules when he drives, such as no one can talk to him unless he says something first. He cracks me up.

"All right, kids," Luke said as he dropped us off. I think he gets a really big kick out of calling us kids. "I'll be back by ten. Have fun." Then he gunned the engine and peeled out of the driveway.

Stacy answered the door. "Hi, guys," she cooed at all the boys. She was wearing a green-and-white dress and green heels. Stacy has heels in every color, I think. She immediately put her arm through Sheck's and led him into the foyer. Sam, Nick, and Jason followed.

Al, Sabs, Katie, and I were left standing on the front step. We looked at each other, rolled our eyes, and laughed.

"It's going to be a long night," Katie said.

I grabbed Allison's arm and we walked in together. Katie and Sabs were right behind us. By the time we got inside, Stacy and the guys were nowhere in sight.

"How rude!" Katie exclaimed.

"Well, we knew Stacy was going to act weird. She always does," Sabs said. "Besides, we're here, aren't we? I'm sure Stacy can't be too happy about that."

Just then the door to our right suddenly opened. Mr. Hansen walked out into the foyer where we were standing. I didn't know about anyone else, but he was definitely not someone I wanted to see right then.

"Hi, girls," he said pleasantly. "I'll take your coats. Everyone's leaving them in here." He gestured behind him to the open door. "The party's downstairs. Just go straight ahead and down the stairs on your left."

We gave him our coats and headed down the hall. It was strange, but Mr. Hansen didn't seem concerned about the loud music or anything. Could that possibly mean that Horrible Hansen, our principal, might be a little cool? What a thought!

The basement was packed with kids. I couldn't believe how many people were there. It seemed as if everyone from Bradley Junior High had showed up. I didn't see Sheck anywhere.

The Hansens' basement was paneled with wood, and there was a thick gold carpet on the floor. There were big, long tables set up on one side of the room with chips, soda, cookies, pizza, and cake on them. This was definitely a weekend for eating. I was going to gain ten pounds if I didn't stop chowing soon.

"Hey, there's Angela," Sabs said, pointing out a girl who played in the band with her. "I'll be right back." Before we knew what was happening, she was buzzing across the room.

Scottie Silver came up behind Katie and put his hands over her eyes. Scottie is in eighth grade, and he and Katie are both on the ice hockey team at school. He acted as if he hated her when she tried out for the team, but then he actually asked her out a couple of times.

"Hey, Katie, what's up? I didn't know you were going to be here," he said. Katie smiled at him. "Hey, come over and say hi to Flip." Scottie pulled Katie over to the food table. It figured the hockey players were hanging out there. Katie looked at us helplessly, as Scottie grabbed her hand and led her away.

Al and I just looked at each other and laughed. Katie and Sabs are so social. I could spend an entire party talking to only one person, and Al is always a little shy when there are a lot of people around.

"Al, you look great," I complimented her. I meant it, too. Since her experience modeling for a fashion magazine called *Belle* a few weeks ago, Al was really looking good. Not that she hadn't looked good before, but she never used to give much thought to what she was wearing. Tonight she had on black leggings, black flats, and a big white shirt buttoned all the way up to the collar. *Beautiful* was the only word to describe her.

"Thanks, Randy," Allison replied. "So do you. Red looks great on you. You and Sheck make a great couple."

I looked at Allison, startled. "What are you talking about, Al?" I asked in surprise.

"You guys look great together," she repeated. "Don't worry, Ran, he doesn't like Stacy. You know that. You can tell he really likes you."

I laughed, or tried to laugh. "Al, he's my best friend. Of course he likes me," I retorted.

"Randy, you know that's not what I meant," Al said.

I changed the subject. It made me a little uncomfortable talking about it. "Hey, let's get some soda, okay?" I moved toward the table and poured a glass for myself and one for Al. Then we walked over next to the stereo and sat down on two empty chairs.

"Did I tell you I decided to stay in Acorn Falls, at least for another year?" I casually asked her, taking a sip of soda.

"What!" Allison exclaimed. "You know you

didn't tell me that." She looked as if she was about to hug me, but stopped herself. "I'm so glad," she finished.

I leaned over and gave her a quick hug. "I am, too."

"I can't wait until you tell Sabrina and Katie," Allison said. "They're going to be so excited!"

Stacy came over and reached between us to turn off the stereo. It was as if we weren't even there. "Okay, guys," she announced. "I just wanted to let everyone know we're going to start dancing now." Then she put a new tape in and turned the music up even louder.

I rolled my eyes at Allison, who giggled, and then turned to scan the crowd. I caught Sheck staring at me from across the room. Suddenly he started moving toward us. I watched as he pushed people aside in order to get to the corner where Allison and I were sitting. Stacy was standing next to me, and I could feel her straighten up as she caught sight of Sheck making his way across the room. She obviously thought he was coming over to ask her to dance.

Instead, he bowed in front of me, asked, "May I have this dance, madam?" and handed his empty soda cup to Stacy. I could hear Allison giggling as

Sheck grabbed my hand and pulled me out into the middle of the room. No one was dancing yet, but that didn't bother Sheck. He loves to show off on the dance floor.

"Hey, Sheck, do me a favor?" I yelled into his ear over the music.

"Anything for you," Sheck answered, grinning. "You don't even have to ask."

"Go ask Allison to dance, okay?" I asked, looking back to where Allison was sitting next to the stereo chatting with Naomi Wolfe from her social studies class. Knowing Al, I thought, they were probably talking about the project they were doing for school.

"I won't let you go," Sheck joked as he grabbed my hands and started dancing again.

I laughed, but didn't start dancing. "Come on, Sheck. I mean it."

"Okay, okay," Sheck said. "Actually, I really don't mind at all. I've had my eye on her all night and was looking for the right opening. Maybe you could introduce us." He winked at me when I punched him in the arm, but he squeezed my hand and walked over to Allison.

I noticed there was a glass door at the end of the room that probably led outside to a patio. I needed some fresh air after all that dancing. I walked over and slid the door open and stepped outside. It really wasn't that cold out. I hugged myself and looked up at the stars. I had to admit that I actually liked Acorn Falls. I was happy with my decision to stay.

I don't know how long I stood out on the patio, but soon I heard the door behind me open. I didn't turn around.

"I'm going to miss you," Sheck said, as he walked up beside me. "Allison told me you decided to stay."

I nodded. What could I say to him? I was really going to miss him, too.

"Well, you'll still come visit me, won't you?" he asked me softly.

I turned and looked at him for the first time. His eyes were so green.

"Of course I will," I reassured him.

He reached out and touched my cheek. "It won't be the same without you, Zak," he said and leaned forward and kissed me really quickly on the cheek. That was really weird. Maybe Allison was right and Sheck does like me.

Suddenly Sheck whispered, "I'll never survive without you, Randy. How will I make it through the month until I see you again?" Then he grinned at me. He grabbed my hand and tried to pull me toward the door.

"Come on, Zak," he pleaded. "Let's go back in."

"Go on in, Sheck," I said. "I'll be right there."

Sheck shrugged, and then said, "Okay, as long as you promise me about twenty more dances."

I laughed again and agreed. I would have promised him two hundred dances.

As soon as I walked back inside, Sabs and Katie came over to me with Allison right behind them. I knew just by looking at the expressions on their faces that Al had told them about my decision to stay. It was kind of nice to know that it made that much of a difference to them.

"I couldn't wait," Allison said before I could even open my mouth.

"I knew you'd never be able to leave us," Sabs added with a grin.

"Randy," echoed Katie, "I'm so glad you're not going back."

Allison just nodded, her brown eyes sparkling.

"You guys are the best!" I announced loudly as I reached out to hug all of them at once. "And Acorn Falls is a pretty great place, too."

Don't Miss
GIRL TALK #5
IT'S ALL IN THE STARS

At the end of the day I went back to my locker to get my dirty gym clothes. As usual, one of my socks was missing. I stood on my tiptoes to search the top shelf. But instead of finding my missing sock, I found an envelope with my name written on the front. I opened it and unfolded the cutest little note on pink stationery. It had a little red heart sticker on it. My heart leapt at the first line:

My Dear Sabrina,

I can't stop thinking about you. You are like a beautiful flower. I can see your face in all my dreams. I know that someday we will be together. Till then, my love, here is my heart.

Your Secret Admirer

I immediately felt my famous body blush beginning. When that happens I feel like I'm about to burn up and my whole body gets red and blotchy. I sure hoped my secret admirer wasn't around to see. It was just like my horoscope had predicted — *a good day for phone calls, letters, and love.*

LOOK FOR THESE OTHER AWESOME
GIRL TALK BOOKS!

Fiction

MORE GIRL TALK TITLES TO LOOK FOR

Nonfiction

ASK ALLIE 101 answers to your questions about boys, friends, family, and school!

YOUR PERSONALITY QUIZ Fun, easy quizzes to help you discover the real you!

BOYTALK: HOW TO TALK TO YOUR FAVORITE GUY